THE
PIRATE OF
FATHOMS DEEP

The Pirate of Fathoms Deep
Tales of the High Court 2
By Megan Derr

Edited by Samantha M. Derr
Cover designed by John Coulthart
http://www.johncoulthart.com/
Map designed by Raelynn Marie
http://becausethatswhatido.tumblr.com/

To everyone who thinks they aren't good enough.
You are.

THE
PIRATE OF
FATHOMS DEEP
TALES OF THE HIGH COURT 2

MEGAN DERR

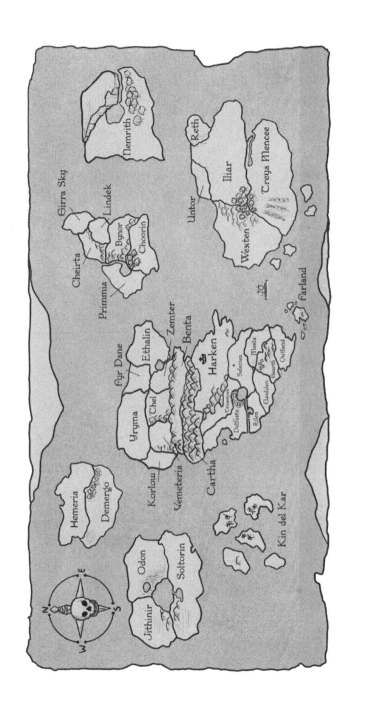

CHAPTER ONE

Lesto whimpered as something jarred, knocking his head against a hard surface. Moving—he was moving. Carriage? No, that didn't feel right. Cart, maybe. That seemed more likely. It jerked again, and he definitely was lying down, head thunking against the bottom of the cart whenever it went over a rock or pothole in the road. How in the Pantheon had he wound up in a damned cart?

His thoughts came slow and heavy, like wading through a cold, muddy river.

They'd been at a tavern—that was his last clear memory. He and the soldiers he'd brought along from Fathoms Deep had stopped at a tavern to eat, the large one located two-days' ride north of Jethamor City. They'd been talking about how good it would be to return home after weeks of trying to sort out the mess that had resulted from a Harken trade ship running ashore, every last hand, mercenary, and passenger on board long dead by swift, brutally effective means—mercenary work, but no mercenary that worked for the Harken Empire. Stranger still, half the people on board had been missing their right hand, as though someone had gone through and chopped them off. Lesto really didn't want to know why, but he was probably going to find out eventually and spend the rest of his life sorry he knew.

Definitely the work of an enemy abroad, but so far, they'd not been able to figure out which one, or why they'd slaughtered the crew and passengers of a Harken imperial galleon but left all of the valuable cargo. None of the thirty-three passengers had been notably powerful or wealthy, so it likely hadn't been a professional hit of any sort, though that possibility hadn't been completely eliminated.

Lesto cringed as they went over another deep pothole and his head knocked so hard he felt close to throwing up.

Drugged—he'd definitely been drugged, and heavily. Whoever was behind this knew the only way they'd get away with it was to keep Lesto too drugged to move. Though now that he was slowly becoming more aware, he could feel the leather wrapped around his wrists and ankles.

Why in the fucking Pantheon would someone kidnap *him*? That was even stupider than slaughtering an entire ship of Harken citizens. Rene was going to enlist the Three-headed Dragons and rain divine terror across the continent until he found Lesto. Sarrica was going to go straight to arresting people and starting wars and not worry about sorting the mess out until he got Lesto back.

Hopefully Tara and Allen would be able to rein them in, but Lesto doubted it. Nobody would be able to stop him if any of his family was kidnapped. Especially not with Allen and Rene's kidnapping in the not so distant past.

Damn it. He was forty-one, entirely too damned old to be *kidnapped.* Forget Sarrica and Rene. The bastards responsible for this had better hope he didn't get loose. He wouldn't need a weapon to make them regret their choices and beg for death.

Why had they done it? Not for the ransom. There

were better people to kidnap for that. No, this must have to do with the fucking ship. It was too much coincidence that he was kidnapped on his way home from investigating the matter. Though he didn't know why the kidnappers were so panicked. He hadn't figured out a single Pantheon-damned thing.

Lesto screamed as the cart struck something, went up, and slammed back down hard before coming to a halt. He blacked out, but not for long because when he came to, the cart still wasn't moving. Voices, faint but clear, washed over him. Rough informal Harken, which was odd given they were in Gearth the last time he'd been aware of his surroundings, and not many people in Gearth spoke Harken. They clearly didn't speak it natively, which was something, though Lesto wasn't certain *what.*

Fuck, he was too old for this stupid, overdramatic shit. He'd just wanted to finish this last major assignment and then he was going to work on retirement. Jader was more than ready to assume the role of High Commander, and Lesto was long past ready to concentrate on being the Duke of Fathoms Deep instead of High Commander of the Harken Imperial Army.

The voices came closer, and then hands tore away the blanket or whatever it was covering him. It was black out, so clearly they hadn't been traveling long— or they'd been traveling long enough that he'd slept right through day and woken up at night. But that didn't seem likely given how difficult the road was and that his muscles weren't all that stiff yet.

Someone hopped up into the cart.

"Is he alive?" someone else asked.

"Shut up," the man in the cart growled as he

crudely checked Lesto over. "You alive, *cheyio?*"

That was a Gearthish word, and not a nice one. *Rotted bitch* was the most common translation, though Lesto had always had the impression there was more nuance to it than that. Allen would probably know. Lesto might not be a silver tongue, but he knew enough to get by in most places, especially with shit-eating thugs stupid enough to kidnap him. *"Go fuck your poxed mother."*

The man gave Lesto's head a rough shove, setting it to throbbing and spinning again. He laughed meanly. "He's fine. Let's get this piece of shit cart moving again. I want to be at Shemal's place before dawn."

Who the fuck was Shemal? Lesto mentally added him to the list of people he was going to kill or severely maim the moment he worked free of his bindings.

The cart started moving again, and the pissing and moaning from his poor, beleaguered kidnappers gradually faded off as guiding the cart in the dark along a shitty road took all their attention. Lesto closed his eye, let the drugs and the pain drag him back into merciful oblivion.

Sunlight warmed his face when he was next forced awake, the hazy, red-heavy kind he hated because it meant it was time to wake up and leave the comfortable bed he so rarely got to enjoy a full night through. Guess they hadn't been able to keep their dawn deadline.

Two men dragged him out of the cart, still half-wrapped in the musty horse blanket that had been covering him. "Do I get to take a piss at some point?" Lesto asked. They just laughed, which was about what he'd expected, and kept dragging him along up to the front door of a sad looking cottage made of Gearth

Bluestone. That stone went for a small fortune all over the world, but in Gearth itself, it was treated as little better than mud bricks.

And they seemed to be in the middle of fucking nowhere, which was going to make finding help so much fun. Lesto couldn't wait for the moment they let their guard down. He was going to enjoy breaking their fucking faces.

They dropped him on the ground a few paces from the door, the blanket once more falling over his face and miring him in the charming smell of dust and horse and quite possibly piss.

One of the halfwits pounded on the door, and a moment later it creaked open. A deep, sleep-rough voice said, in formal Harken of all things, "What in the fuck are you rank corpses doing on my doorstep? Who the fuck is that? I'm going to remove your nether regions with a splintery spoon and feed them to my goats."

"What the fuck crawled up your asshole and died, Shemal?" one of the kidnappers asked in heavily-accented informal Harken.

"Halfwits like you who won't listen to me when I say: leave me alone, I don't want to play your stupid games anymore."

"Look, we're only here because this poxed cart is broken; it won't last the rest of the haul we have to make."

"That's not my problem. Go get someone else in trouble. I have goats to tend and chores to finish and no time to deal with shriveled dicks like you."

"Fuck you, Shemal, you ain't got no fucking right acting so high and fucking mighty. You're so special because you got a fucking pardon? Piss off. You'll be back to breaking laws as soon as you get tired of fucking your stupid goats."

Lesto stopped paying attention as the argument turned into a fight, and it sounded like Shemal was winning, which didn't surprise him in the least because he remembered vividly just how hard Shemal could hit.

He hadn't expected to ever hear that voice again. His heart pounded in his ears. Shemal couldn't be his pirate. But he remembered that rough-edged voice, like years at sea had stripped the softness from it. Lesto couldn't forget it even if he tried—because he *had* tried. Some things simply refused to be forgotten.

Like a world-turning moment a year and a half ago when Lesto had been called to the pavilion to deal with a group of rowdy pirates who'd been caught, not just with stolen goods, but weapons. He'd told the Pantheon-damned bastards to shut up and settle down, and one pirate had stepped forward with a glint in his eye that Lesto saw too late. Shemal had punched Lesto hard enough to leave his eye blackened for days. The only person to ever hit Lesto harder was Sarrica.

Lesto had been intrigued, and once he'd gotten a good look, he'd been captivated despite all common sense. Shemal's brown skin and the long, heavy locks of dark hair, the cheap hoops in his ear and nose had marked him a native-born Farlander even before he'd opened his mouth and called Lesto a mother fucker. And the colorful tattoos that covered *every* strip of skin had marked him a lifelong pirate.

That should have been the last time he'd seen Shemal, should have been their only interaction. Lesto had laughed and walked off, tried to forget the incident. But Shemal hadn't left his thoughts, and when Lesto had seen him later in the judiciary halls, alone down a side hall returning from taking a piss, Lesto had thrown away caution and sense. One stupid, searing look that echoed his sudden thoughts and he'd surrendered to a dangerous impulse that had resulted in an encounter hot enough the memory was seared into his mind with a vividness that had never faded.

The speed with which Shemal had fled afterward hadn't faded either. At least now Lesto knew the bastard's name. What in the Pantheon was Shemal doing here in the middle of the foothills of Gearth, claiming to be retired?

His stupid heart refused to stop pounding. Probably wouldn't until Lesto's worthless, traitorous mind stopped replaying the delightful, filthy, forbidden things he had done with a pirate still in chains and awaiting trial. Lesto had done a lot of stupid things in his life, but fucking Shemal had definitely taken the dubious honor of number one.

He grunted as somebody knocked into him before they hit the ground with a high-pitched yelp.

"Stay down or I'll finish breaking your face, and it can't afford to get much uglier," Shemal said, speaking Harken again. "I can't believe you've kidnapped a fucking Rilien noble. Do you know what they'll do if they catch you?"

One of the men scoffed. "They ain't going to do shit to us except give us the ransom and go back where the fuck they came from. Lord Bestowen here is going to be our passage to an easy life."

"That's not how it works," Shemal said with a sneer worthy of Sarrica.

Lesto groaned. They thought he was *Lord Bestowen*. No, absolutely not. He refused to believe he'd been kidnapped because the two greatest morons on the continent saw his eyepatch and mistook him for a fat, spoiled noble who made his money on cattle. Had they missed the part where he'd been wearing his Fathoms Deep tunic and had been surrounded by Fathoms Deep soldiers?

"Get the fuck out of here," Shemal said. "Get your damned cart fixed, and if you're not back here by nightfall, don't expect him to be here in the morning. Understand me? And you'd better have my money!"

"Yeah, yeah," the second man muttered, and the two sulked off, whining to each other in Gearthish.

Once they were gone, and the noise of the cart had faded off, Shemal heaved a sigh. Lesto could feel and hear him crouch down nearby, grab hold of the blanket. "I'm sorry about this, my lord. We'll have you home—" He stopped as he threw the blanket aside. *"Corpse fuckers."* He stared at Lesto, recognition, disbelief, and anger filling his face. His eyes were still the most beautiful that Lesto had ever seen, a jeweled teal that put Fathoms Deep teal to shame. "You're still in uniform!"

Lesto blew out a short, huffy breath. "I'm aware."

"I've never seen this stupid lord they thought they kidnapped, but I'm going to guess you don't look anything like him."

"He has an eyepatch," Lesto said, "but it's on the other eye. Could you untie me?"

"Are you going to attack me?" Shemal asked, irritation sliding away as amusement took its place. "I don't need trouble from you anymore than I need it from them."

"If you keep not untying me, you're going to have a whole lot of trouble the moment I get myself free,"

Lesto snapped.

Shemal rolled his eyes, but rose smoothly and vanished into his cottage, reappearing almost immediately with a wicked-looking knife typically used for cutting up fish and other ocean creatures, but favored by pirates for less pleasant reasons. He cut Lesto's bindings, helped him to his feet, and slowly let go when it didn't seem like Lesto was going to fall over. "Come in and sit down."

"First, I'm taking a damned piss," Lesto snarled and stomped off to do so while Shemal laughed.

When he was done with that, Lesto headed into the cottage because as much as he would love to leave, he had no idea where he was, and he wasn't going to get very far thirsty, hungry, and exhausted from a shitty ride in a cart while drugged up on something that had left behind a nasty headache. Though that could have just been the cart. "Where in the Pantheon am I?" he asked, sitting on the rickety stool by a sad little fireplace when Shemal indicated he should.

"Gearth, which you probably knew. About two and a half days of riding from the sea, up in the foothills," Shemal said, swinging a battered kettle away from the fire and pouring boiling water into a bowl filled with some sort of rough powder. It smelled like the ass-end of a drunk cow.

Lesto glared when Shemal held it out.

Shemal lifted his eyes to the ceiling. "Drink the damn tonic, you poncy little palace boy. It'll fix your head."

"I've had about all I can take of being slipped—"

"Shut the fuck up and drink it," Shemal cut in, shoving the bowl into his hands before getting up and stomping over to the little table in the opposite corner of the room, cluttered with cooking tools and little shelves for dishes and other items.

If Lesto didn't know any better, he would think he'd hurt Shemal's feelings. But he definitely knew better. Shemal didn't care about anything but a quick fuck and bragging rights. Lesto hadn't even known his name until now, as the one he'd given to the port authorities had been the usual generic, obviously made up sort of name pirates always provided.

He grimaced at the bowl and drank the contents quickly. It was exactly as foul as it smelled, but that probably meant it wouldn't kill him. The deadly stuff always tasted sweet. Setting the bowl aside, he wiped his mouth with the back of his hand. "Thank you," he said gruffly.

Shemal shrugged, not turning away from whatever he was doing at the table.

Heaving a sigh, Lesto folded his arms across his knees and laid his head on them, tried to call up a map of Gearth in his mind and figure out where he was and where he needed to go. If they were in the foothills, then his kidnappers had likely planned to take him to the point where Gearth, Gaulden, Selemea, and Mesta all collided.

The roads there were clogged and busy, and the market was barely manageable for the poor guards assigned to work it—everybody who joined the imperial army worked the Market of Four for two years. It would be pathetically easy to get a hostage through and onward to wherever they'd planned on taking him. Which was probably to Rilen, so they could demand their damned ransom and be near to hand to accept it. *Halfwits.*

His best bet was to head east into Mesta, to the imperial garrison in Brimin City. It'd be much faster than trying to get to and through the chaos of the Market of Four.

"Don't get too comfy," Shemal said gruffly. "We need to leave sooner rather than later, before those corpse fucking cretins come back with horses and whoever it is they didn't want to admit they were meeting in town."

"Meeting?" Lesto sat up straight again, groaning as his poor, abused muscles protested. Shemal held out a cup of what smelled like apple-flavored mead, and Lesto accepted it gladly, chasing the nasty tonic away with several sips. "Thank you. Who would they be meeting?"

"Whoever it was that told them to do this," Shemal said. "Those two halfwits aren't the thinking type, as you may have noticed. If they were, they'd have realized they've kidnapped High Commander Lesto Arseni of the Imperial Army of the Harken Empire, Duke of Fathoms Deep, and best friend of the High King." He made a face and drank the cup he'd been holding between tightly clenched fingers. So he wasn't quite as calm as he appeared. "How did they manage to get *you*, anyway? I punched the shit out of you once, and you barely stumbled half a step back. I put a lot of swing behind that punch."

Lesto smirked. "Sarrica hits harder than you."

Shemal rolled his eyes. "I have a weaker punch than the High King, wonderful. Anyway, we need to get out of here."

"We?"

"You think they're gonna let me live once they know I let you go? No way, I have worked way too hard

19

and long to wind up feeding wolves now."

Lesto finished his mead. "Why aren't you helping them?"

"Because even when I was a pirate, I didn't hold with treating people like things," Shemal snapped, beautiful eyes going dark, tightening around the ages, his hands jerking. "Unlike the rest of you corp—"

"Corpse fuckers, yes," Lesto drawled.

"You don't get to make light of my anger, High Commander, not when it's your fucking military kidnapping my people to die in your stupid fucking wars."

Lesto lifted his hands. "You're right. That was not my intent, but it little matters. My apologies. For what little it's worth, that's a problem we've been trying to fix. Of late, the High Consort has been helping." He lowered his hands. "I truly am sorry."

Shemal shook his head, took their empty cups away. "Are you up to walking? That's what we're going to have to do until we can obtain some horses, and that will take a few days since we can't go into the village—and their horses are all fat, old farm animals not quite feeble enough to kill."

"I'll manage," Lesto said. Pantheon, when was the last time he'd had to trudge anywhere? He already missed being a spoiled brat. "Let's get moving."

"In a moment." Shemal vanished through a door near the table, and Lesto could hear him rustling and banging around. He reappeared after a few minutes, carrying two satchels. Between them he packed most of the foodstuffs in the cottage—some sausages, half a loaf of bread, and the better part of a small circle of cheese. A few other things, but Lesto didn't see what. Can you carry this?" he asked, holding out one of the satchels.

Lesto took it, slinging it over one shoulder and across his chest. He sorely missed having a sword at his hip. "I don't suppose you have any weapons beyond your fish knife?"

Shemal shook his head. "Wasn't allowed under the conditions of the pardon."

"When has that ever stopped any of you?" Lesto asked, casting him a look before leading the way out of the cottage.

Shrugging, Shemal turned down a small footpath that led further into the scrubby foothills. "Where would I get even a half-decent weapon out here, anyway?"

"Why *are* you out here?"

"I'm finished with my pardon, not that it's any of your business," Shemal said. "There was work here someone was willing to give to a former pirate."

Lesto frowned. That didn't make sense. The standard sentence for pardoned pirates, especially the kind caught smuggling weapons out of the country, was three years hard labor somewhere well away from the sea. There were always estates that needed more farmhands and such. There'd be nothing for Shemal to do all the way out here in the middle of nowhere.

He'd actually recommended Shemal to be shipped to Fathoms Deep, which always needed more labor. His holdings were enormous, and it took every pair of hands available to get the planting and harvesting done even remotely close to on time. Never mind everything else that went into farming. Four percent of all the wheat used by the empire came from Fathoms Deep land. The majority of the rest of his not-insubstantial income came from turning out the best mercenaries in the empire, even if Fathoms Deep itself had turned into Sarrica's private guard.

But when he'd returned from dealing with Benta, it was to hear that Shemal had refused the offer from Fathoms Deep and gone elsewhere. Combined with the way he'd vanished almost immediately after they'd fucked... Well, Lesto knew when someone had decided he was a bad idea best swiftly forgotten.

It wasn't like he could blame Shemal. No half-intelligent criminal would choose to stay in the same room as the High Commander. Very few persons at all, in fact, stayed in the same room as him for very long. Those who did generally wanted the power and forty thousand crowns a year that would come with marrying him.

"If you're done, why wouldn't you go home—?"

"That's enough with the questions," Shemal cut in. "More walking, less talking, Commander."

Lesto heaved a sigh, but he could hardly argue. Pantheon knew it took all his energy and concentration to keep moving. He was tired, hungry, sore from being stuck in that stupid cart, and more than a little banged up from the same. Undercutting all of that, draining his energy with worry and fear, was the constant fear for his men—had they been drugged, or had they been killed?

Then there was Sarrica, Rene, and the others. If they didn't already know he was missing, they would very soon, and he had no fucking way of letting them know he was all right. Damn it.

Fretting about it incessantly wouldn't help, though, so he turned his attention to his reluctant companion, who still cut a fine, distracting figure in well-fitted breeches and a slightly too-small shirt, left unlaced to accommodate his broad shoulders, showing off muscle and tattoos. He moved like every pirate Lesto had ever known: deft and quick and sure-footed, like a goat happily scaling a sheer cliff face.

He'd been even more distracting standing bare-chested, his feet in manacle, calling epithets and curses to Lesto's exhausted, frustrated guards. Lesto had known better than to get too close, he'd been a victim of rowdy, nothing-to-lose pirates on several occasions as a young soldier. He'd done it anyway, and gotten a black eye Sarrica would never let him forget.

Then he'd risked his life and livelihood to indulge a stupid impulse. Years of youthful stupidity had nothing on that single, too-brief moment of skin and heat and need. He had stupidly thought, for reasons he still couldn't explain, that everything would be different. That *Shemal* would be different.

And he'd been played for a fool, gotten exactly what he'd deserved for acting so stupid and reckless.

Lesto stumbled, didn't catch himself in time, slammed down on the rocks, and scraped open his knees and palms. Swearing, he leveraged himself to his knees and grimaced at his hands, picked out a few small bits of rock and dirt.

"Going to make it, old man?"

"Who the fuck are you calling old?" Lesto said. "You're not that much younger than me."

Shemal grinned as Lesto looked up. "Still younger, so you're still older." He extended a hand.

Ignoring it, Lesto slowly stood and brushed off his knees. "I'm going to stop going near anything to do with water and pirates. All it brings me is trouble."

The grin faded, and without any further words, Shemal turned and resumed walking. After several minutes, he said, "We should be at a reasonably safe campsite by dark, if you can walk that long. We can stop in a couple of hours to rest, but not for more than a few minutes."

"I'll be fine," Lesto snapped.

Silence fell after that, the sort of heavy, miserable silence Lesto hated, but it was better than making the mistake of lowering his guard and letting Shemal make a fool of him again.

The sooner he was home, the better.

As promised, they stopped after a couple of hours. Lesto unslung his satchel, found a jug of water, and gratefully helped himself. It had a strong mineral taste, but it was better than a lot of water he'd drunk over the years. He passed the jug to Shemal and pulled out food. There was enough to keep them for three days, which, according to what Shemal said, would suffice until they reached the next village.

He should have been able to remember the name of it, but he'd never spent much time in Gearth and certainly not in such remote parts. He couldn't wait to never see them again.

When he'd eaten several bites of food and felt moderately less inclined to murder the whole world, Lesto asked, "I don't suppose those two halfwits said anything about my men? We were dining at a tavern when they grabbed me. Slipped something in my beer, I think."

"They said they were all drugged, and I can't see why they'd lie about that," Shemal replied stiffly. Then he paused, a bite of cheese halfway to his mouth. He looked up, a deep frown cutting into his face. "What do you mean you were dining at a tavern with your men? They took you while you were surrounded by

Fathoms Deep? Wearing Fathoms Deep uniforms? With everyone calling you Commander?" He slipped into Farlander, muttering several words that required no translation, then abruptly switched back to Harken to say, "How they are still alive after all these years of bungling, I will never understand."

Lesto heaved a sigh. "I'm more bitter that I'll never live down being successfully kidnapped by those two halfwits only to be rescued by the same bastard who once punched me in front of half the imperial army." Sarrica would howl about it for hours and bring it up at least three times a day for half a year.

A brief grin stole across Shemal's face, but he ducked his head to hide it and shoved the last bites of food into his mouth. "Come on," he said a couple of minutes later, his levity gone like it had never existed in the first place. Lesto was clearly not the only one who couldn't wait for him to be back in Harken. "The more we walk, the less likely they are to find us."

"They'll be on horses, according to you," Lesto said as he slung the satchel back over his shoulder and fell into step behind Shemal. "We stand no chance on foot."

"I wish them luck figuring out which path we took. The ground around here is hard, dusty, doesn't hold footsteps well. I doubt anyone in their group can track worth a damn, if the best kidnappers they were willing to pay for were those half-dead minnows. They also have to get that stupid cart fixed, and they won't realize they no longer need it until too late. Hopefully, anyway." Lesto didn't need to see him to know the fleeting grin that was there. "Regardless, I think we've bought ourselves enough time to get somewhere more useful."

"Let's hope," Lesto said. Once he reached a town large enough to have an imperial garrison, he would be safe—and once more in a position to knock people over until he was satisfied there were no more halfwits standing. The world's most irritating kidnappers had taken his weapons and money, but they'd left his uniform and rings: the Fathoms Deep signet and the imperial signet with his name carved inside. Those were worth infinitely more than money, and it was all to the good they hadn't seemed to realize that.

A matter of weeks and he'd be home again and could put this whole stupid, ridiculous mess behind him, ghost ships, kidnappers, pirates and all.

CHAPTER TWO

Hours had passed, but Shemal's heart had yet to stop doing its best to beat right out of his chest.

His fingers skated across his stomach, the tattoo there burning with memory and the fear that somehow Lesto would see it. Then what would Shemal say?

A hundred hundred times his mother had warned him he would one day get exactly what he deserved for being a restless, uncaring devil. *Only the ocean can do as it pleases without consequence.* A man who acted with all the arrogance of the sea always got his comeuppance in the end.

But what did Shemal have to fear? He had lost count of the successful raids he'd been part of over the years. He was well-seasoned and still in good shape. He'd once punched the High Commander of the Imperial Army and lived to tell the tale. Not that he had told it. He should have been locked away for the rest of his life but had been given an abbreviated pardon sentence and was a free man with a clean record. What did he have to fear? Nothing.

Except the way his heart raced whenever he so much as thought about Lesto. The way all it took was one look for Shemal to agree to whatever Lesto suggested. The way, even after months and months of trying, he couldn't forget the way it felt to have Lesto beneath him, his rough fingers bruising Shemal's skin as he gripped tightly and begged for more.

The way he was trying to go respectable on the futile, flimsy hope that Lesto might give him a chance at being more than a dirty secret.

And remembering that soured everything. He had managed to convince himself he was content with fucking the High Commander and walking away. Then he'd been informed he'd been offered pardon work on Fathoms Deep land. No doubt expected to report directly to His Grace periodically. Shemal had heard of such scenarios a thousand times before. He wasn't interested in being some lord's kept whore.

Fool him for thinking Lesto might be better than that.

Yet he'd tried to go respectable anyway, and now he here he was, risking his fool neck to save the man who'd unknowingly been dictating Shemal's life and driving him mad for the past year and a half.

Shemal stared across the short space between them to where Lesto had already fallen asleep. He'd fought it, but after a long few days of kidnapping, walking, and scowling in a way that was far sexier than it had any business being, staying awake was a lost battle. Shemal was impressed Lesto had lasted as long as he did.

Then again, it must take a person of incomparable mettle to command all the military forces of Harken *and* be a near-constant presence at the side of the High King. Back home, the term for people with such fortitude was *storm tamer.* It wasn't a term used lightly. It definitely wasn't a term applied to thieving, bloodthirsty, unworthy Mainlanders.

But the first time he'd seen Lesto, striding across the yard, jangling sharply with every measured step, everyone else shifting and moving to revolve around him... The yard had been a roiling mass of chaos, all tired, angry guards and scared, volatile prisoners. They'd been one step away from turning into a battleground. Lesto had stepped out and a calm had followed in his wake. Hundreds of eyes had followed him, filled with respect, admiration, and far filthier thoughts, but Lesto hadn't seemed to notice.

He'd approached Shemal's group and told them to shut up and calm down. Shemal had punched him just to see what he would do. To watch him break the way imperious, arrogant Mainlanders always broke when faced with an actual challenge. To prove Lesto didn't deserve all the fawning admirers surrounding him. Lesto *hadn't* broken, though. He'd fallen back half a step, stared at Shemal with disbelief and respect . He'd laughed as he told the guards to haul the fucking pirates away. He'd strode off like a rushing tide sweeping across the sand and leaving it smooth.

Shemal swallowed and looked away, stared up at the stars, absently marking his location by them and aching for something familiar to anchor him. Since being captured and charged with piracy and smuggling—he hadn't known about the weapons, neither had most of the others, which was why they'd been let off with pardons—he hadn't found a place to settle that felt right.

He certainly wasn't welcome back among old friends, though that was an overgenerous word for them since, like any Mainlander, his fellow pirates were more than happy to throw an Islander overboard if they thought it would get them out of trouble.

Shemal hadn't felt bad about giving up the worst of the lot, not by a grain. That had gotten him free and clear in less than a year, and he'd been trying to sail a proper course ever since.

Just his damned luck that the first bit of trouble to come his way in so long also brought with it the whole reason he was trying to behave in the first place. He wished they'd managed to kidnap the stupid earl they'd actually been after.

The clenching in his gut revealed the lie, not that he'd really been fooling himself.

He turned his head again, wished there was more than moonlight to see by. Come daylight, Lesto would be too rested and aware for Shemal to get away with staring.

The stupid bastard looked good with an eyepatch, like some chief who was the pride of his clan, had protected them through several storms and beaten off imperial corpse fuckers, and had more lovers than he could keep up with and more children than he could count.

Picturing Lesto with other lovers made him feel like he'd drunk saltwater for hours straight. Given all the time that had passed and, well, *Lesto*... He probably had a lover. A real one. Not some stray pirate he'd have to keep secret.

Swearing softly, Shemal sat up, folding and crossing his legs, resting his elbows on his knees and sinking his fingers into his hair. Once they obtained horses, it would only be another day at most before they were somewhere that had a garrison. After that, Lesto would go back to his life and Shemal to his.

Three days to the nearest village, and an additional day to reach a well-sized town. Four days to...what, exactly?

"Why am I not surprised you're one of those who never fucking sleeps?" Lesto asked, voice rough with sleep and not at all unpleasant. A hundred wistful thoughts spun through Shemal's mind, but he pushed them away. "What's keeping you awake? I doubt anyone is going to find us tonight. They don't strike me as the sort of people to work that hard. If so, they'd have kidnapped the correct person, or at least found a better cart."

Shemal laughed. "Even if they weren't that lazy, which they are, the chances of them finding us are about as likely as finding a gold ring lost at sea. I didn't mean to wake you."

"I never sleep long, especially when I'm not in my own bed," Lesto said. He pulled the satchel he'd been using as a pillow close and pulled out cheese and bread, breaking the bread in half and handing a portion to Shemal. "So why are you awake?"

"I don't sleep well in strange places either. Too many years of waiting for trouble to appear on the horizon."

Lesto snorted. "What trouble could possibly find you out here?"

"Incompetent kidnappers and angry commanders," Shemal retorted, grinning when Lesto snorted. "I almost wish I could see their faces when they figure out what they've really done, but I'd prefer to stay as far away as possible because there's no telling how dangerous their client is." He sighed and took a bite of sharp, salty cheese and soft, faintly sweet bread. It wasn't the flat bread cooked over open flame that they ate back home, piled with fresh vegetables (and fish when he couldn't avoid it), but it wasn't the worst he'd ever eaten. Almost any food was better than none. "So what were you doing all the way out here?"

He almost withdrew the question when Lesto's mouth flattened. It wasn't like he'd expected an answer. But just as he started to ask a different question, Lesto said, "A ship washed up on shore, all hands dead—murdered rather brutally. The cargo wasn't touched, though. It was like the mercenaries climbed aboard, murdered everyone, and slunk away again.

A chill ran down Shemal's spine. "Were their throats slit with a serrated blade? Were some of them missing their right hands?"

Lesto's head snapped up. "How did you know that?"

Shemal swallowed the lump of cheese suddenly stuck in his throat, fumbled with his own bag until he found the water they'd refilled just before deciding to stop for the night. "I only came across them once, when we were stuck in port because of a storm. This was across the sea in Treya Mencee. A group of men dressed in black, with white hands dripping blood as their crest. They're called the Hands of Death. A not much talked about group of mercenaries who work unofficially for the royal family. If that entire ship was slaughtered by the Hands of Death, then somebody pissed off a Treya Mencee royal, and they've sent a warning."

"I've never heard of them," Lesto said. "I know all the mercs that work for Treya, and I've never heard a whisper of them."

"You wouldn't," Shemal said flatly. "That's not how they work. I wouldn't know except I was with a rough crew at the time because my last ship had been waylaid by port authorities and they were my only way home. Once the storms let up, we were gone, and I never saw shadow nor splash of them again. But they stick in the mind. If I were you I'd figure out who or what was on that ship that'd piss off the Treya Mencee royal family, and I'd do it quickly."

There were several beats of silence then Lesto said gruffly, "Thank you."

Shemal shrugged, wished he knew why his stupid heart had started thudding madly again. He was thirty-eight years old, far too old to be acting like a kid with his first infatuation.

"So how's life as a free citizen?" Lesto asked, though the question sounded a bit sour.

"Boring. I really hate goats. But it's better than accidentally smuggling weapons. As my mother would say, everything settles at the bottom eventually."

Lesto snorted softly. "That sounds more ominous than I think it's meant."

Shemal flashed a quick grin. "I guess it loses something in the translation."

"Unlike your insults, which seem to carry over well enough. I'm not sure what you get up to on those islands when your favorite insults are mother fucker and corpse fucker."

"That just conveys our low opinion of Mainlanders," Shemal retorted.

Lesto grunted at that, but did not otherwise reply.

Had Shemal said something wrong? He'd thought they were having fun. *Flirting,* his stupid, unhelpful mind pointed out. Shemal ignored it. What point was there to it? He wouldn't be a dirty secret, and someone like Lesto wouldn't—couldn't, if Shemal felt like being fair—have him any other way. Whatever Shemal's hopeless fantasies about making himself respectable enough, it would never happen. An

Islander with a criminal past was never going to be anything but a tool or an amusement to a Mainlander duke, especially when that duke was half a step from the throne.

If only Shemal could figure out how to get his logical, reasonable thoughts to bite. It wasn't fair he was constantly at war with his own damned mind.

"Given you have such a low opinion of us, I'd think now that you're a free man, you'd have hightailed it back to Farland."

Shemal shrugged. "If I wanted to stay at home, I would have never left, or returned a long time ago."

"You seem to hate it here more," Lesto replied.

"I don't hate it," Shemal said. "Don't get me wrong, there's a long list of *corpse fuckers that I'd love to turn into shark bait*, but most people don't mean any harm. Everyone just wants to get on with their day with as little trouble as possible. As to back home... Well, I am the youngest son of a youngest son. It's our *sacred duty to stay out of the way* unless we're doing something to help everyone else. I have no desire to spend the rest of my life serving my brothers, sisters, and all their children. By this point, there's a flock of grandchildren too." He made a face. "So I'll just stay here."

Lesto made a soft noise that Shemal could not decipher. "Not much for children?"

Shemal peered at him through the dark, *something* in Lesto's voice crackling along his skin. There was a weight to the question, as careful as Lesto had been to ask it idly. Why should it matter? What was the right answer? But even Shemal knew the only answer he could give was an honest one. Lying about such things always led to disaster. "I didn't say that. I like children,

34

but if I'm going to spend my time raising them, I prefer they be my own, not those of my halfwit brothers more interested in the process than the results."

That got him a laugh. Shemal flushed with pleasure. It wasn't the same kind of laugh he'd gotten after punching Lesto. This was a real, genuinely amused, probably reached that pretty gray eye kind of laugh. If things were different, it was the kind of laugh to chase with a kiss.

Things weren't different, though, and the few paces between them may as well have been an ocean.

Still, he'd always been in favor of piling on the self-torture. "What about you, High Commander? How many miniature Commanders are running around commanding armies of dolls and wooden soldiers?"

"None," Lesto said, "but I was thinking of changing that in the next year or so."

Did that mean he did have a lover? Or, more likely if he was planning to have kids that soon, a spouse? Shemal didn't know if he wanted to laugh or scream or cry. "I'm sure they'll be adorable little terrors straight from the Penance Realms."

Lesto laughed again, though it didn't sound quite as happy as the first one. "So I've been told." He shoved a last bit of cheese into his mouth and stood. "If we're not going to sleep, we may as well keep walking."

"In the dark? Unless your one eye has some magical properties that my two lack, that doesn't seem a very sound notion," Shemal replied, though he climbed to his feet as he said it and swung his satchel across his chest.

"There's moonlight enough, and the ground isn't treacherous. Unless you pirates can't see in the dark even a little."

"I'm not a pirate anymore," Shemal muttered, but he obeyed the unspoken order to take the lead. Stubborn fucking halfwit.

Unfortunately, Lesto proved to be a *correct* halfwit. Shemal wasn't certain why that surprised him. He doubted Lesto was ever wrong about anything.

Except maybe about fucking pirates while they were still under arrest and awaiting sentencing, but Shemal didn't want to think about Lesto believing that had been wrong. It hadn't felt wrong, except for the bit where it could never be more than the once.

Unless he wanted to settle for being a lord's kept whore, which no, he'd rather return home and become a glorified babysitter.

They stopped for a break as the sun was coming up, settling with their backs against a large tree, Lesto facing the road and Shemal to his right , facing the way they'd come.

He didn't remember falling asleep, but the sun was well in the sky when Lesto shook him awake. "Mmf—" Shemal groaned. "No, I don't want to."

"Oh, stop whining," Lesto said gruffly, but Shemal could hear the smile in his voice and that was enough to pop his eyes open. Fuck, every time he looked at Lesto, it was like getting punched in the gut. His good eye was like a storm cloud mixed with gleaming silver. "What's wrong?"

"Nothing," Shemal said, shaking his head. "I didn't mean to fall asleep." He fumbled around to get leverage to stand, but his hand slid on dew-slick moss and he wound up falling right back down on his ass. "Mother fuck—"

Lesto's laugh drowned out the curse, and before

Shemal could react, he was grabbed around the arms and hauled to his feet. That put him far too close to Lesto and his dumb, handsome face. "Are you certain you're all right?"

Shemal swallowed. "I'm fine. Let me go."

Lesto's levity faded, hurt taking its place in the moment before his face closed down and he was once more the cool, remote High Commander. His hands fell away, but the feel of them lingered on Shemal's skin as he stepped away from the tree and back onto the road.

He'd just pulled out the jug of water when Lesto said, "I can't figure you out."

Shemal looked up with a scowl. "What's to figure out?"

"Oh, I don't know," Lesto snapped. "You fucked me like there was nothing else you'd rather do then left with all the speed of a serious regret. I arranged a comfortable pardon term for you at Fathoms Deep only to return to find you had vanished without a word. One minute you look at me like you want to kiss me, and the next minute you look like you'd rather slit my throat. Which one is it?"

Dropping the jug back in the satchel before lobbing it at Lesto's head, Shemal replied, "I think we have more important things to worry about than your bruised ego. I'm sorry I didn't leap at the chance to be your dirty little secret, Commander. Get over it." He stormed off down the road, swallowing futilely against the rock in his throat, pressing a hand to his chest like he actually thought that would get his heart to slow to a less alarming pace.

And he should have expected it, he really fucking should have, but he still yelped with surprise when

Lesto grabbed him from behind and yanked him back. Shemal hit the grass to the side of the road with an *oof* and stared up at the man looming over him, more turned on by Lesto's sheer presence than he would ever admit. Even when he wanted to climb to his feet and punch Lesto again, there was an underlying desire to kiss him at the same time.

"When did I ever say I wanted to keep you as my dirty secret?" Lesto demanded.

"How about the whole sending me to be a laborer on *your* lands where I no doubt would have had to report personally to you every week or so?" Shemal's lips curled. "I know you *corpse fuckers* think we're all ignorant *Islanders* with *a few too many holes to be a useful bucket*, but I wasn't born yesterday. I've seen it happen a thousand times, *you eager mother fucker.*"

Of all things, Lesto *laughed.* Forget punching him, Shemal was going to kick him in the balls. "You do the same thing High Consort Allen does when he's agitated or overworked."

"What are you talking about?" Shemal snapped.

Turning serious again, Lesto said, "You speak more than one language at a time, snapping back and forth so seamlessly, it's obvious you don't know you're doing it." Lesto crouched down beside him. "Stop calling me a mother fucker. It's in poor taste to speak ill of the dead, and my mother was a wonderful lady when she was alive."

Shemal flinched. "Sorry."

Lesto shook his head. "I never intended to keep you a secret. I set up the pardon work at Fathoms Deep because we always need the help and we treat laborers well. I send a lot of people there, as many as I can—especially Farlanders, who get mistreated more than most. If you'd *stayed* that afternoon, I would have told you what I had in mind. You have a lot of damn nerve accusing me of shame and secrets when you're the one who couldn't leave that room fast enough. But at least now I know where we stand." He stood up then bent and hauled Shemal to his feet, unslung the bag across his own chest, and thrust it at him. Shemal oofed again as he caught it, barely avoiding dropping the damned thing on his feet. "Thank you for your assistance, but I would prefer to travel on alone from this point. Fair winds and swift waters." He turned and strode off, vanished around the bend in the road before Shemal could even begin to gather his thoughts.

The stupid, infuriating, corpse fucking bastard son of a crusty fisherman. Why was he *walking away*? Argh, spare him the confounding idiocy of Mainlanders.

Settling the second bag across his chest so it fell on the opposite hip as the other one, Shemal went storming after Lesto, nearly at a run before he finally managed to catch up. At the last moment, he opted for a lunge-tackle, sending them both crashing to the hard-packed ground.

"What in the Realms—" Lesto bellowed, jerking and twisting, trying to buck Shemal off—but only winding up thoroughly pinned in place. "The moment you let me go, you are dead," he hissed.

Shemal returned the glare full measure. "You don't get to decide all by yourself that the conversation is over. Am I going to get to defend my actions the way I let you defend yours? Or is the high and mighty commander the only one who gets a fair chance to say everything on his mind?" Shemal started to say more, but stopped short at the hurt and resignation that flickered across Lesto's face. He must be exhausted to the point of near death because surely it wasn't normal for someone like Lesto to wear his emotions so plainly.

"This high and mighty commander is done," Lesto said flatly. "Let me up, fishbait, or that is exactly how you'll end the day."

"Why did you leave before letting me explain myself?" Shemal demanded. "I listened to you, why won't you listen to me?"

"Because your fear of being my dirty secret doesn't have anything to do with the day you fucked me!" Lesto snarled, and Shemal was so taken aback by the vehemence of the words that he let down his guard— and went flying backward to land awkwardly in the grass.

He stared up, a touch awed and breathless, as Lesto rose. Damn it, was there a single moment of the day where the man was not magnificent? Even dirty, scruffy, and verging on murderous, all Shemal wanted to do was stare and touch.

"I can see where you misunderstood my attempts to help in sending you to Fathoms Deep, and I am sorry," Lesto said. "But you didn't know about that when you fucked me. It hadn't even been arranged yet. I'd only just thought of it. We weren't at such great risk you had to rush out almost before you'd finished coming. You're not the only one who knows the signs, and I know damned good and well when I'm being used. Got yourself some fine bragging rights, didn't you? Hundreds of people would love to brag they punched me and fucked me and wound up a free man at the end of it, but you're the only one who *can*. You must fucking love that."

Shemal opened his mouth, closed it again, too overcome by shame and regret to know what to say. They'd seen each other in that hallway, and Lesto had snuck him away... Everything had happened so fast, and felt right and overwhelming... He'd gotten scared and run away. He'd felt dangerously close to hooked and hadn't known what to do about it.

Lesto turned away, but not before Shemal saw the naked pain and disappointment on his face.

His stomach churned. Was that what happened to Lesto? People saw the Commander? The Duke? It made sense. People in Lesto's circles were always aware of those sorts of things in a disturbingly shark-like way.

He couldn't deny there'd been a bit of a dirty thrill behind punching and fucking High Commander Lesto Arseni. The memories that constantly tormented him, however, had nothing to do with *haha, got one over on the fucking High Commander* and everything to do with the way Lesto had felt beneath him, his wrists pinned by Shemal's hands, legs wrapped around Shemal as he'd begged breathlessly for more and moaned so sweetly as he came. The only thing Shemal had hated was not hearing Lesto say his name, and he'd been on the verge of giving it. That was when the panic had set in, and Shemal had fled before he said or did something stupid—well, stupider than fucking Lesto in the first place.

It had never occurred to him to *brag* about any of it. Even if he'd wanted to, who would believe him? But he hadn't wanted to—plenty of people had seen him punch Lesto, but gossip like that always faded off eventually. And the rest... the rest was his, a bittersweet memory that haunted his dreams and shadowed his every waking thought. It had never been something to discuss with others, let alone brag about.

Climbing to his feet, Shemal once again went hurrying after Lesto. Mother Ocean knew what he was going to do when he reached him. *If* he reached him— Lesto could move fast when he wanted. And that after days of kidnapping, endless walking, little food, and barely sleeping.

Shemal never wanted to see him at full strength. He doubted he'd survive.

And now was not the time to ponder how much fun that energy would be in a proper bed with all the time in the world to enjoy it. Lesto, well-rested and uninhibited... Mother Ocean, what would that be like? If their one crude and hasty encounter was enough to engrave itself on Shemal's mind, how devastating would it be to take his time? To learn and savor all that had been hinted at in their one encounter. To know more about the man who'd taken a hard punch with a laugh and apparently always tried to take care of Islanders.

To know the man who'd taken more of a risk, and offered more trust, than Shemal had ever realized?

By the time he managed to catch up to Lesto, he could barely breathe, and thinking was flat out impossible.

Lesto tried to jerk away as Shemal grabbed his arm and turned him around. "What in the Panth—"

Shemal kissed him, grabbing the back of Lesto's neck with his free hand to try to hold him in place.

The attempt failed miserably, but Lesto didn't walk off again, so maybe it wasn't a complete failure. "What do you think you're doing?"

Even two steps away from killing him, Lesto was still breathtaking. Shemal might have a problem, but he couldn't bring himself to care right then. He had too much else to be worried about. Like being completely honest. He was infinitely more comfortable with lies and half-truths. But the idea of hurting Lesto again was unbearable. "It wasn't a matter of bragging rights. You're not *that* special."

Lesto's eye narrowed, and Shemal could feel the muscles in his arms flex and tense.

"I was scared, all right?" Shemal continued hastily. "I'm a worthless pirate and I *punched* you. I've been places where people like me would be arrested or even killed for looking too long at someone like you. But there you were, sneaking me away, and—" He swallowed, throat suddenly feeling scraped raw. "I think I was allowed to panic a bit. I never—I never said anything. To anyone. It wasn't about that. I punched you just to see what you'd do. I never expected the rest. It never even occurred to me it was possible until it happened."

Lesto stared at him, gray eye intent, his frown as fierce as a hurricane. Shemal loved and hated that they were the same height. It would be so much easier to look away if he were shorter or taller.

Finally Lesto gave a soft huff and pulled away. Disappointment twisted through Shemal like sharp thorns—but it burst into shock and relief when Lesto yanked him in and kissed him like he had the first time. All at once, nothing held back, like a wave crashing over a ship and knocking over the sailors not smart enough to anchor themselves.

Shemal whined, high and sharp and needy, fisting his hands in Lesto's tunic as he kissed back like a man lost at sea who'd finally found land. The most frightening part of Lesto was that *anchor* and *land* were exactly how he'd felt from the moment he'd taken Shemal's punch and met it with laughter and admiration. Like he could take whatever was thrown at him and never break or give up. Why that was so heady, Shemal didn't feel like figuring out.

He'd rather sink deeper into the kiss, wrap his arms around Lesto, and enjoy relearning all the little things he hadn't been able to forget for the past year and a half. Mother Ocean knew he'd tried. Even after days of mistreatment and endless walking, Lesto still had appeal. The warmth of his mouth, the rough scrape of his facial hair, the deft, knowing fingers that twined in Shemal's hair, and the way he didn't protest in the slightest when Shemal took control of the kiss, plundering that willing mouth like it was the last thing he'd ever do.

Drawing back, voice more ragged than he liked, Shemal said, *"Mercy of the sea, you're* more distracting than I remember."

"I don't understand half of what you're saying," Lesto replied with a faint, shockingly pretty smile. "I suppose I'll have to learn."

If Shemal had thought his heart was beating madly before, he was proven horribly wrong. He mustered a scoff. "Mainlanders aren't good enough or smart enough to speak the language of the nine seas."

"There are ten seas."

"Apparently Mainlanders can't count, either," Shemal retorted, a grin overtaking his face. "Why you split the Heart of the Sea—"

"It's called—" Lesto broke off, shook his head. "Never mind. Stop distracting me. Can I dare hope you're not going to run away again?"

Shemal rolled his eyes and slowly let go of Lesto, missing the feel of him the very moment it was gone. "Where would I go? No ship will have me, I just pissed off a whole lot of dangerous people by taking you from them, and I can hardly drag all my problems home. If I try, my father will turn me into *shark bait.*"

"That's a term I actually know," Lesto replied. "Come on, you were right in that this really isn't the time or place."

"Then why did you bring it up instead of waiting until we reached a safer place?"

"Because it was driving me mad." Lesto looked away then sighed and added, "I wasn't certain you'd stay around long enough once you'd dumped me off. I just wanted—no, needed—to know."

Shemal's chest felt so tight he was half-afraid something was going to pop. "My mother always warned me I would get exactly what I deserved one day."

Lesto's brow furrowed. "What?"

"Nothing," Shemal said, face heating. "So what am I supposed to do now?"

"Come back to Harkenesten with me, and we'll figure out the rest from there," Lesto replied gruffly. "Promise you won't vanish on me again."

Shemal swallowed, gave a jerky nod. "I promise."

That got him another genuine smile. It lit up Lesto's face, brought more silver to his eye, made him look younger.

Yeah, Shemal was definitely getting exactly what he deserved. After almost four decades of never holding still, he'd managed to stumble across someone who made him forget how to move.

45

He was probably going to panic later when he could no longer avoid thinking about it, but for the moment, it was as easy as moving with a tide to steal another kiss before falling into step beside Lesto as they continued their journey.

CHAPTER THREE

The village came into view as the sun was nearly set, a small cluster of mud and grass houses, a couple made of actual stone in the middle of the loose circle they formed. Lesto could smell roasting meat and bread on the air, and the evening breeze blew thin trails of smoke all about.

He'd never been so happy to see civilization in his life. He was dirty, hungry, exhausted, and stretched thin to the point of tearing. The only things keeping him together were one, the knowledge that in one more day, two at the most, he would be back in the fold of the imperial army and in control again.

Two was Shemal, who'd gone from a sour memory to awkward reunion to a heady rekindling of hopes Lesto had tried his damnedest to stamp out. Shemal, who'd promised not to run away again and agreed to return to Harkenesten Palace with him.

Lesto had never minded his life the way it was, had always, in fact, been perfectly happy with it and would have continued to be so, whatever memories occasionally haunted his dreams. But he couldn't deny he enjoyed the idea of Shemal becoming a part of it. Something about him tugged at Lesto to the point of madness. Made thoughts of retirement and settling down and family more solid.

"I smell food," Shemal said with a groan. "Thank the *mashta* ocean."

Lesto smiled faintly. Shemal and Allen would

probably get along, though it would probably take some time for Shemal to feel comfortable around Allen. "I think the only thing I want more is a bath and clean clothes."

Shemal glanced over his shoulder and flashed a small, faintly shy grin that Lesto could just see in the fading light. "You arrange the bath and food; I'll do something about clothes."

"Deal," Lesto said, and as they reached the center of the village, he split off toward the scraggly little tavern that even the smallest villages tended to have because it was a place for locals to gather, and where travelers would flock and make keeping an eye on them simple. There was no inn, but arranging to bed down in a stable or storeroom wouldn't be hard.

He stripped off his filthy Fathoms Deep tunic so he wouldn't draw too much attention, as the people after them could come looking at any time. Tucking it beneath his undertunic, wedged at the small of his back, he stepped inside. The tavern smelled like shepherd stew and the dark, nutty bread common in Gearth, a bit like smoke underscored by the odor of sweat that existed wherever people gathered often over a long period of time.

It took only minutes to flag down the tavern owner and arrange for baths and food, as well as secure a place they could sleep for the night. Once he'd handed over coin, given to him earlier in the day by Shemal, he headed out the back door of the tavern and down a short hall to where the bathing room was located.

As in most places in Gearth, bathing was a public thing. In cities, there were large, ornate halls with giant pools of hot and cold water. Here, there was probably a nicer bathing house for the village and this smaller, simpler one for the rare traveler.

But it was clean and well-cared for, had a deep bathing pool, a large washing area with plenty of soap, rags, and razors, and the other side had stacks of clean towels. It was very far from the worst he'd seen in a long life of soldiering.

He stripped off his filthy clothes and threw them in a bin meant for garbage. The only thing he retained was his eyepatch, which he carefully scrubbed clean and set aside to dry. When that was done, he set to work on the rest of him. He scrubbed down twice then shaved and trimmed his hair, sadly neglected while he was preoccupied with the ship.

After that, he gave himself a final scrubbing, and by the time he'd rinsed off, he almost felt human again. Reaching up, Lesto touched the ruins of his right eye, destroyed by an assassin's dagger in a swift, brutal, dark-of-the-night fight. Every now and then, on the longest, hardest days, he still woke up remembering the pain, or momentarily confused that something didn't feel right.

The injury wasn't pleasant to look upon either, but hopefully it wouldn't be so off-putting that he lost the pirate he'd just gotten back.

He slid into the bath with a long groan, settled on a bench, and let his head rest against the high edge. Against his chest, gleaming beneath the water, were his rings: the Fathoms Deep signet and the ring of the Imperial High Commander.

Picking them up, he ran his thumb over the Fathoms Deep ring, which bore the skull and swords, and on either side of the band were compasses. Framing the skull was a circle, the top half a string of coordinates, the bottom half the family motto in a shorthand version of formal Harken.

He dropped the rings again, sank deeper into the water with another groan.

"I think I'm insulted that hot water gets more responses out of you than I ever did."

Lesto laughed. "The hot water isn't under arrest and in danger of being caught at any moment." He sat up and twisted around to look at Shemal. "You'll get your chance once we're clean and fed."

Shemal's eyes widened then sharpened with an eager, hungry look. Almost as gratifying was the way he seemed to pay no mind at all to Lesto's damaged eye. If it bothered him, Lesto hadn't noticed.

And then he forgot what he was thinking about as Shemal stripped and all that lovely, colorful skin was bared.

Lesto's heart jumped into his throat when he saw the tattoo on Shemal's abdomen that definitely had not been there the last time he'd seen Shemal. The Fathoms Deep crest. Lesto's crest. "When did you get that?" he asked softly.

Shemal flushed. "After I finished my pardon service. I—I wanted to be respectable, so I wouldn't have to be a dirty secret. The tattoo was a reminder of why I was trying."

Lesto made a rough, ragged noise. "You were always respectable. Given my family lineage, I'd have a lot of nerve taking issue with a pirate. And the imperial army has done much the same things as pirates, mercenaries, and smugglers—the only difference is that we do it with permission. Get clean."

Shemal obeyed with surprising meekness, scrubbing as thoroughly as Lesto had before finally joining him in the water. He settled close by, reached up slowly to rest his fingers against Lesto's scars. "You rather look like a pirate yourself. There's not a one of us who isn't marked up somewhere." He grimaced faintly.

Probably over the scars on his back—not as extensive and horrible as the ones on Allen's back, but nothing to scoff at either. The only 'kindness' granted to Shemal in his whipping was that it had been done by an expert doing a job, not some cretin enjoying the power and suffering.

"Well, it's an improvement on accusing me of fucking my mother," Lesto said with a faint smile.

Shemal laughed and didn't look even a bit sorry.

Lesto was no rude, impatient youth eager to get off at every opportunity. The very idea of trying to act that way was exhausting. The chance to savor a few kisses, to be close for a little while—that idea was infinitely appealing. Lesto lifted his own hand as Shemal's fell away, rested his fingertips against Shemal's cheek.

Shemal drew a sharp breath. "It-it feels wrong to call you Commander, but I don't think I've ever used your name."

Lesto huffed a soft laugh. "Use it now." He didn't give Shemal a chance to do so, however, but closed the remaining distance between them and kissed him. Softly. Slowly. Leisurely. No desperate haste. No biting anger. Shemal tasted salty and sweet, reminiscent of the taffies Lesto had eaten incessantly as a child.

That was the only childlike comparison to be made, however. As Lesto vividly remembered from the day he'd surrendered to a dangerous impulse and snuck Shemal into an empty room, pulled him to the floor, and all but demanded that Shemal fuck him.

In retrospect, it wasn't hard to see why Shemal had panicked and made assumptions about what Lesto was planning to do.

Fingers fluttered against his chest, and Shemal drew back just enough to breathlessly whisper, "Lesto."

Lesto groaned. "Shemal. I didn't even know your name."

Shemal drew back a bit further, eyes the color of a summer sea. "I was always sorry about that. I would have liked for you to know."

"I know now." Lesto leaned in to kiss him again, drawing it out, determined to memorize every last little thing about the way Shemal felt and tasted and kissed. They stopped only when their growling stomachs became impossible to ignore. Withdrawing with a quiet laugh, Lesto said, "Let's go eat."

Shemal smiled and stood. Lesto reached out, helpless against the need to touch the beautiful tattoo. "I like it."

Snickering, capturing his hand and keeping it firmly against his abdomen, Shemal said, "A fancy lordling commander likes to see me wearing his mark, fancy that."

Lesto flinched, jerked his hand away, and stood. "Sorry, that wasn't—" He broke off and turned to climb out—and bellowed when Shemal yanked him back and sent him splashing into the water. Clambering up, sloughing water, Lesto glared. "Why do you keep doing that?"

"Because I can," Shemal said with a grin. "Because you won't punish me for it. Also it's irritating when you try to run off."

Lesto's glare didn't lessen. "I can think of a few

fitting punishments I'd like to administer."

Surprise rippled across Shemal's face, his jaw dropping slightly. Then he grinned as mischievous as Lesto had ever seen. "Why, Commander, I'm shocked."

"I very much doubt it," Lesto retorted.

Shemal's easy grin turned into a slow burn, and Lesto didn't have to ask what he was thinking. There was only one memory that potent shared between them, after all. Shemal surged forward, shoved him back so hard Lesto slammed into the wall at the back of the bath. It wasn't remotely comfortable, but he could not bring himself to care. It was infinitely more distracting to be pinned in place by a ravenous pirate.

The air was so thick and wet it was hard to breathe, and Lesto was overheated from being in the water too long. He hadn't behaved like an impatient youth in a long time, but fuck, Shemal suddenly made him want to try.

Drawing back, chest heaving, Shemal licked his lips and said, "Let's go eat, because I'm going to need the energy for all the irresponsible behavior I have in mind."

Lesto laughed and let Shemal help him out of the water. They dressed quickly and thankfully, his eyepatch was mostly dry. He hadn't been looking forward to everyone gawking at him more than they already would. The clothes were slightly too small and smelled faintly of bitter mothflowers, but they were clean and comfortable, which was all he really required.

His boots weren't so pleasant, so Lesto carried them back down the hall and handed over another bit to have them cleaned.

They then settled at a table in the back corner, and a serving boy brought them large bowls of shepherd's stew, a platter of bread and butter, and cups of dark beer. Lesto had just started on his second bowl when he heard the familiar jangle-rattle of armor and sword belts. The smile he'd just given Shemal faltered, soldier training rushing back to the fore as a group of ten rough-edged men stomped into the tavern.

And he didn't have even a dagger to work with, damn it.

The soldiers were all pale-skinned, which was strange. Pale skin was only predominant in a few kingdoms in Harken, and they weren't so prevalent an entire band of soldiers was likely to share the same old-milk skin tone. That usually indicated foreigners, a theory further substantiated by their strange armor— red leather trimmed in gold. Flashy, the kind of armor that was less for protection and more for intimidation.

They stepped further into the room, eyes skimming over the diners. The stick-thin man with cold eyes who seemed to be in charge went still as his gaze landed on Lesto. Looking pleased, he turned to the others and said something in a low tone, the words soft and rolling, almost lyrical.

Treyan, they were speaking Treyan. That explained why they were all pale and skinny. What were a bunch of Treya Mencee mercs doing in a two-hut village in Gearth?

Lesto dismissed them, went back to his stew, murmured low, "I think we might have trouble, but I'm not sure. A group of Treya Mencee mercs is a far cry from the pair of halfwits that grabbed me. They've no business being in such a remote place as this without imperial escort."

"Maybe somebody figured out who it is they've actually kidnapped."

"Treya Mencee mercs kidnapping me would start a war," Lesto replied. "They don't want that. Treya Mencee's contracts with Harken are too lucrative."

Shemal gave him a look. "You're assuming Treya Mencee is sanctioning this."

Lesto frowned, mind spinning as he tried to sort out what could possibly be going on. It was too much coincidence that such a strange, dangerous group would appear in a tiny village shortly after Lesto and Shemal. And Treya Mencee had come up regarding the strange murders on that ship, too.

He glanced briefly around at the way the men had scattered—sitting so they could easily stand, blocking all exits. The serving boy who'd been tidying had vanished, and such strange guests should have drawn the woman who owned the place, but she too was notably absent.

Reaching beneath his tunic, Lesto removed the chain around his throat and slipped the rings free. He pushed them across the table. "Put those on."

Shemal frowned as he picked the rings up. He started to shake his head, but at a glare from Lesto, he obediently slid them on his fingers. The same warmth that had unfurled and spread through Lesto at seeing Shemal's tattoo returned at seeing his family ring on Shemal's finger.

He tucked it away to enjoy later, when they were safe again. "If something happens to me—don't give me that look, we know I'm the one they're after—do whatever it takes to get to Sarrica, Allen, or Rene. Get to a garrison and the soldiers will see to it you reach the palace. If they question you having the rings, tell them I said they know where I'll bury them if they don't listen to you. If Sarrica or my brother Rene get tetchy, tell them I said I was going to explain the coordinates to you."

"You don't make any sense," Shemal said. "It's not nice to say something mysterious right before we're about to get our asses kicked by a group of fish belly thugs."

Lesto grinned. "The short answer is I trust you as much as I trust Sarrica and Rene."

"Ah." Shemal smiled at him, soft and pretty. "I suppose I can settle for..." He trailed off as two of the mercenaries approached their table, his smile turning sharp and cold as he said something to them in Treyan. Shemal really was at least a little bit of a silver tongue.

The shorter of the two mercenaries replied, and as had been the case on countless other occasions, Lesto didn't need to know the words to understand the insult.

Shemal's smile grew even sharper, a look in his eyes that Lesto knew far too well. Then his arm flashed out, hand clutching his fish knife. He drove it into the throat of the shorter mercenary. As that one reeled back and collapsed, Shemal stood, grabbed his chair, and slammed it into the other one.

Lesto slid out of his chair to kneel on the floor and deftly relieved the dead man of his sword and one dagger. By the time he stood, the rest of the bastards were coming at them, and the small tavern crowded with tables and chairs made for a poor battleground.

He kicked a table into a cluster of three, which gave him a chance to bring one of them down. The other two shoved the table out of the way, came at him hard, and Lesto heard too late the one that came up behind him, jerked but not enough to avoid the thrust entirely, fire bursting along his side as the edge of the blade caught and sliced.

Shit. He slammed the dagger into the gut of the man behind him, grabbed him by the collar, and threw him at the other two before rushing them, stabbing one, snapping the other's neck.

Pain shot up his thigh and he looked down to see someone had tried to get in a last thrust—thankfully missing the place that would have left him bleeding out in seconds.

Lesto dropped, suddenly too hot and dizzy and struggling to breathe. Shit, shit, fucking *shit.*

"Stupid fucking—" Shemal broke off and pounded across the room. "Lesto!"

Dragging his eye open, Lesto looked into Shemal's. "The fucking bastards had poisoned blades, I think. At least one of them. I'm not—"

"You can't die," Shemal said, voice cracking. "Damn it, I'll go find a healer."

Lesto managed a ragged laugh even as he slumped against Shemal. "You won't find one here. You have to get me to the nearest garrison. If I live that long. They're the only ones..."

Everything went black then, and the next time he managed to open his eye, it was still black. But he could make out stars, he thought, and from the way they were moving and the familiar pounding of hooves on dirt, they were on a horse.

Sarrica was going to have even more to make fun of him for, getting his ass kicked by Treya Mencee thugs. Lesto was too old for this shit. He was done being in charge of Sarrica's damned army. He would never understand Nyle's desire to go back into the fray when he'd had such a wonderful life. It wasn't Lesto's place to judge, but he wasn't certain he'd ever entirely forgive his brother either.

He drifted off again.

The third time he stirred, they were still on the damned horse. "Shemal…"

"Almost there," Shemal said, voice trembling. "You stupid, useless Mainlander." He lapsed into Farlander then, and Lesto smiled. Or thought he smiled. He wanted to smile. He could so easily see now why Sarrica was so fond of the way Allen lost track of his languages sometimes. It was probably far too late for Lesto to learn a new language, but it didn't seem right not to make the effort.

When Lesto woke yet again, he felt decidedly more lucid. He was also in a bed—in his private chambers at the imperial garrison in Brimin City.

He tried to sit up and immediately regretted moving, pain slicing up his side and across his ribs, cramping down and making it impossible to breathe for a brief but terrifying moment. What in the fucking Realms had those buggering bastards done to him?

At least he was alive. Lesto looked around his room, which was as stark and clean as ever. A spare set of armor hung on a stand in one corner of the room, a large trunk beside it holding weapons and other equipment. A dark blue tapestry depicting a three-headed dragon hung over the window. From outside came the usual din of the garrison and more faintly, the noise of the city.

Someone had propped him up slightly, at least. Fuck, what was wrong with his side? Had the sword gotten him that badly? Gritting his teeth against the pain, Lesto carefully got the blankets out of the way.

Thankfully, the cramping-can't-breathe moment didn't come again, just a slightly stabbing ache that wasn't even close to the worst pain he'd ever dealt with. That dubious honor belonged to his eye.

He grimaced at the wound revealed, a nasty gash lurid with redness and black healer thread, glistening with the sharp, pungent ointment smeared over it all. From the look of the damned thing, it had been some sort of rough-edged blade. No wonder it had hurt so much. Reaching beneath the blankets, he could feel a similar wound on his thigh.

Pantheon, he was definitely too old for this nonsense. He wanted to be home worrying about crop yields and contemplating finding Shemal to do something inappropriate in his private sitting room.

Where *was* Shemal? Hopefully headed for Harkenesten like Lesto had told him, but anything could have happened while Lesto was unconscious. At the very least, a few days had passed. His head felt too wooly to be anything but still feeling the aftereffects of sedation.

He looked to the side of the bed, gritted his teeth again, and leaned over enough that he could snatch up the large, gold bell sitting right at the edge of the bedside table. He hadn't rung it more than once when the door flew open and an unfamiliar, alarmingly young soldier stepped inside. "You're awake! I'll inform the captain at once! I'm glad you're doing well, Commander!" The door slammed shut as abruptly as it had opened.

Lesto set the bell down and sighed at the ceiling as he settled back in the bed. Who in the Pantheon had put a fresh recruit on his door? Whatever, he'd sort that matter out later. He rested back against his pillows, closed his eye, and tried to sort his thoughts out.

He still could not explain why they'd been attacked by Treya Mencee mercenaries. He'd been kidnapped by men who had thought he was some fat, officious, useless Rilien noble. What the fuck did Treya Mencee have to do with that? This must all go back to the ship, but damned if he knew more than that.

Thankfully, he was spared thinking about it for a little while longer as the door creaked open and Mishi, the garrison healer, stepped into the room and shuffled across the room to him, a large, looming, black-skinned woman behind him—Ofera, the garrison captain.

Mishi smiled in his warm, grandfatherly way. Lesto had seen him put an arrow in a man's eye from two hundred clicks; he wasn't fooled by that smile for a moment. "Good afternoon, Commander. We've been searching frantically for you. Leave it to you to show up half-dead, carried in by a pirate. Never do anything by half—including injuries. Lucky for you, it was bubble fish poison."

"Lucky," Lesto drawled, though in fact it was. He and Sarrica had both been victims of bubble fish poison when they were young, one of several reasons he wished Sarrica would heed Lesto's orders to take bodyguards wherever he went.

But the one good thing about bubble fish poison was that, once survived, it was a lot harder to be too severely affected by it again. Given how much time had passed since he'd accidentally ingested it, he wasn't terribly surprised it had still caused him trouble—but it hadn't been fatal, which it would have been otherwise.

"That certainly explains why I feel like old shit," Lesto replied. "Where is Shemal? What is going on? Have I missed anything important?"

Mishi rolled his eyes. "Let me look over your wounds before you start in with barking orders and sending everyone scurrying."

"Speaking of sending people scurrying," Lesto said as Mishi threw back the blankets and began to examine him. "Why is there some ten-year-old watching my door?"

Ofera grinned. "He's your greatest admirer, Commander. Begged for the honor, sweet as you please."

Lesto groaned and pinched the bridge of his nose. "No. Absolutely not. I'm not putting up with that again." He grunted, leg jerking. "Damn it, man."

"Oh, quit your fussing," Mishi replied. "You're missing an eye—you can handle me poking at your leg."

Lesto glared. "Stop dragging on about it."

Mishi just clucked his tongue and kept going at the exact same pace he'd been working. Lesto heaved another sigh. Honestly, the man poked and prodded just to be an ass; what was there to look at? The leg was stitched and itchy enough it must be healing properly.

He looked at Ofera again. "Where is Shemal?"

"He left yesterday morning. You've been asleep a little less than three days. Got here late a couple nights ago. You've been in and out ever since. He refused to leave your side until he knew you were stable, and I think he only left at all because he was doing as you told." She smiled. "He seems quite fond of you, Commander."

Lesto grunted but didn't confirm nor deny it. "I want a group sent back to the damned village to look over those fucking mercenaries."

"Already sent them, the very moment I knew what had happened. I also sent hawks out to Harkenesten and Sufta to notify everyone you'd been found. I wouldn't be surprised if Master Shemal encountered His Majesty on the road."

If Sarrica had left the palace to join the search, Lesto was going to fucking kill him. Slowly. With his bare hands. "He'd better not."

"We all know you're never that lucky, Commander."

"Tell me something I want to hear before I demote you for being a pain in my ass," Lesto replied.

Ofera laughed, folded her arms across her chest. "The team that was with you to sort out the ship is downstairs feeling sad and dejected. I have people all over Gearth to start sorting out this damned mess, and they should be sending reports by this evening. My message to His Majesty included the warning that Treya Mencee is up to something. For the moment, we're at the waiting part of everything."

"Wonderful," Lesto muttered.

Dropping her arms, smile widening, Ofera added, "Deputy Commander Jader sent a message to say that if you want to retire, there are better ways to do it."

"Deputy Commander Jader can kiss my ass and had best watch his tone because I haven't handed off authority quite yet."

Mishi snorted as he finally withdrew. He rummaged through his healer bag for a moment then handed over a small twist of powder. "You'll certainly survive to terrorize everyone for a little longer. I don't suppose I can convince you it would be best to stay in bed for another day or two?"

Lesto gave him a withering look.

"That's what I thought," Mishi said, rolling his eyes again. He walked around the bed and poured a cup of water from a pitcher on the table. Dumping the medicine powder in it, he held it out. "Drink it, or I'll pull healer's rank and see your sorry ass is tied to this bed since you won't voluntarily stay in it like a sensible person."

"Says the man who once walked three miles on a broken leg," Lesto retorted.

Mishi packed up his supplies. "Yes, when I was young and stupid. Been stuck with a limp ever since. Drink the damned powder."

Making a face, Lesto nevertheless obeyed, downing the bitter drink quickly and setting the cup down with a hard clack. "Are you finished harassing me now, you old blood drainer?"

"I'll be finished making your life miserable only on the day I die. Stop trying to beat me to it." Mishi squeezed his shoulder, smiled faintly then limped off across the room, closing the door quietly behind him.

Lesto turned to Ofera. "Would you get me some clothes?"

Ofera nodded and went over to the wardrobe in the corner opposite the armor and trunk to pull out one of the spare sets of clothes that Lesto always kept there. If he'd learned nothing else in a lifetime of soldiering, much of it commanding, it was to keep clean clothes in as many places as possible.

He slid slowly out of the bed, privately relieved that the medicine was already taking effect and dulling the worst of his pain. Ofera returned with the clothes and helped him dress, and for the first time in several days, Lesto felt like himself again.

Thought it was increasingly a version he'd like to leave behind. He was *tired* of all this—the violence, the pain, the exhaustion, the weight. Long past time he handed over command and enjoyed the rest of his life as a spoiled brat noble.

"Let's go," Lesto said. "I want food, and then I want to hear everything in detail from the moment Shemal brought me here to when I woke up."

"Yes, Commander." Ofera was silent as they left the room, but as they headed downstairs and into the bustle of the main portions of the garrison, she said, "So about you giving Master Shemal—"

"Shut up," Lesto said. "I don't want to hear it. Not a word. I'll throw you and everyone else in this place into the stocks, don't think I won't."

"Yes, Commander," Ofera repeated, and Lesto didn't have to turn around to know she was grinning. "He's very pretty."

Lesto did turn around that time, summoning the glare that normally sent soldiers running, but all it got him was more grinning and a bit of loud, vibrant laughter.

"The whole garrison knows. It would have been obvious to a dead man that's he's sweet on you, and you kept saying his name in your sleep." Ofera said. "You may as well accept it's become general knowledge that the High Commander has been caught—by a pirate no less."

Snapping back around, Lesto resumed heading down the stairs. "Mishi should have mentioned that. It would have convinced me to stay in bed." Reaching the bottom of the stairs, he bellowed for someone to bring food to his office as well as all available reports on the current matter. "I also want to know where the fuck every last Treya Mencee citizen in Harken is living, especially titled and military. If you can drag them in without fuss, do it. If it's going to cause a fuss, try asking nicely first. But I want them hauled in, whatever it takes." When he got confirmations of his orders and had sent soldiers scattering like startled cats, he turned left and swept down the hall to his office.

CHAPTER FOUR

Shemal was going to be sick. All over his horse. It didn't matter he hadn't eaten for most of a day, and that meal had been little enough. Whatever remained in his stomach was going to come up and splatter the horse and then the soldiers would snicker and cast him even more looks than they already were. He had the sinking feeling they all knew of his feelings for Lesto and were making fun of him. He could understand what the lieutenant said, but the others had such thick Rilien and Tricemorien accents that he'd given up figuring out what they were saying. But he didn't need to understand them to know when he was being made fun of, not when he was an Islander surrounded by imperial soldiers.

Had Lesto woken up yet? Was he all right? They'd said he was on the mend, but something could still go wrong. Shemal was still mad at himself for not better dealing with the mercenaries. He should have been faster. Stronger. *Something*.

He knew damn good and well Lesto could handle himself, that someone less experienced than Lesto wouldn't have lived long enough to worry about poison, but it didn't ease his guilt. If he'd been just a little faster, he might have gotten to those bastards in time to protect Lesto.

Now he was racing up the road as fast as the horses could safely manage in the company of men who kept sharing looks and snickers. Was it really so laughable that he cared about Lesto? Or were they laughing because they knew something he didn't?

But Lesto wasn't the type to take a lover if he already had one, and he'd sworn he had never intended to keep Shemal a secret. Lesto had given Shemal his rings. The imperial ring alone granted alarming amounts of power. But the Fathoms Deep ring... That was infinitely more precious because it was clearly an old ring, an heirloom, and Lesto had trusted it to him.

So let them laugh all they wanted at the stupid, smitten pirate. All their mockery wouldn't take Lesto away. He hoped.

Exhaustion washed over him, but Shemal pushed it back. If he could stay awake for two days straight while a storm tried to tear apart the ship and half the crew was sick, he could stay awake for this. He would deliver his information to the High King, rest, and then return to Lesto as quickly as possible.

How remained a challenge, since he doubted anyone would care about him once he ceased to be useful, but he'd figure something out. For the moment, he'd focus on the immediate goal: reaching the High King.

But that goal was simple enough, and little effort was required for keeping one eye on the road. It was far too easy for his thoughts to drift back to Lesto, worry and affection whirling about, and under all of that, anxiety about what would happen to him when they finally made it to Harkenesten.

It was easy enough to agree to accompany Lesto there, easy enough to say he wouldn't run...but what was a penniless reformed pirate supposed to do in the imperial palace? A reformed pirate who was also an

Islander, the lowest of the low in the eyes of most of the Harken Empire. Would Lesto really still want him once he was surrounded by peers again? Would the High King and Lesto's family even permit the relationship? There must be better prospects awaiting someone as powerful as Lesto.

"Ho, there! Stop in the name of the High King!"

Shemal jerked from his thoughts, looked up to where a cluster of six guards were arrayed across the road. They wore the same uniform as the four men surrounding Shemal, and his group didn't seem alarmed as they drew to a stop.

The man in the center of the new group looked at Shemal. "Are you Master Shemal?"

"Well, I don't think anyone has ever tacked on the 'master' bit, but yes, I'm Shemal."

A smile twitching, the man said, "His Imperial Majesty the High King has arrived at the imperial garrison in Sufta City and bids you come at once to see him there."

"The High King is *here*," said the lieutenant in charge of Shemal's group. "Why in the name of the gods is he here? The Commander is going to skin him alive."

The other man's twitching smile broke into a full grin. "Especially once he hears High Consort Allen came along as well."

"Oh, merciful Pantheon, the Commander is going to kill all of us," muttered the lieutenant, and around them, the others added their own curses and sighs. "All right, let's get moving then. At least now we don't have to ride all the way to Harkenesten. I was not looking forward to that."

The soldiers who'd stopped them all laughed and

wheeled their horses around, falling around Shemal. He felt boxed in, just this side of under arrest. "Is there a reason you're caging me? I'm not going to run away."

The man in charge of the second group moved closer to him, extended a hand. "I'm Captain Matameia of the Sufta Imperial Garrison. His Majesty sent me personally to see to your safety. We're not keeping you in; we're keeping everyone else out."

"Oh," Shemal said faintly. "Um. That's not how it usually goes. I'm, uh, Shemal, but I guess you know that. Shemal shey Variago."

"Shey? That's not the bit Farlanders usually use."

Shemal shrugged, scrubbed the back of his head. "You probably know 'frey' and 'vrey.' Those indicate whether you're high or low in your family, more or less. Shey means I stand apart. So my, um, poor standing with the empire doesn't reflect on my family. Anyone who hears shey knows I act without my family's sanction, but I'm not so terrible my family has rejected me."

"Captain, you can pester him later, come on."

Matameia laughed. "Yes, yes, you're right. Let's go, Master Shemal. If a single hair of you is harmed on my watch, the High King will remove all my hair at the neck." He didn't give Shemal a chance to reply, just bellowed the order to move and heeled his horse forward.

And they were off again, racing to beat the wind. But when they came to a split in the road, they headed left, veering toward Sufta instead of taking the road that was a direct line to Harkenesten.

By the time they reached Sufta, night was falling and Shemal was about ten minutes from falling off his horse and sleeping wherever he landed.

Sufta was one of the largest cities in Selemea, and the only powerful city that wasn't also a port. If the High King was already all the way to Sufta, he must have left the moment he knew Lesto was missing and traveled quickly.

Of course, the High King being in Sufta meant that instead of being days away from seeing him, Shemal was only moments. He tried to tamp down on growing panic as they rode through the city gates, a soldier racing ahead of them blowing a horn to clear the streets. Several minutes later, they pounded through the enormous black stone gates of the imperial garrison and came to a halt in a large courtyard half-filled with soldiers and horses.

Shemal dismounted, head ducking against all the eyes he could feel. The last time so many soldiers had looked at him, he'd been getting his release papers stamped. Before that, it was after he'd punched their commander.

Mother Ocean, he hoped none of them recognized him. The imperial army must have tens, if not hundreds, of thousands of soldiers. Surely none of those who'd seen him punch Lesto were here—and it had been a year and half since that day, what were the chances they'd be here *and* recognize him?

Matameia gave him a nudge and Shemal followed him through an archway, past several torches, into the great hall of the garrison. More soldiers stared as they strode briskly through, up a set of stairs at the back and down two short hallways to a set of double doors marked with the imperial griffons. The guards stationed there, a towering man and a short, young woman, saluted Matameia and pulled the doors open.

Shemal wanted to turn and run, but Matameia

kept right on going so he had no choice but to follow suit. The doors slammed shut behind them with a terrifying echo.

"Your Majesties, I present Master Shemal," Matameia announced to the two figures sitting at a small table scattered with food and papers.

The one on the left, big and handsome, with scars across his forehead and the left side of his face, and a close-cropped beard, looked up from the papers he was reading. Reputation alone marked him the High King. "Thank you, Captain. You're as reliable as always. You're free to go."

"Yes, Majesty." Matameia saluted and strode out, clapping Shemal on the shoulder as he passed.

The doors opened and closed again. Shemal swallowed, keeping his eyes on the floor.

"So you are Lesto's pirate."

Shemal jerked his head up. How did he already know? "Majesty?"

The High King huffed impatiently. "You're the pirate who rescued him, the one who recognized him and got him away from the kidnappers. If the missives we've received are to be believed."

Oh. Shemal's knees almost gave out in relief. "Yes, Your Majesty."

The High King's eyes narrowed, but all he said was, "Tell us everything from the beginning, so we can hear it in full detail."

"Yes, Your Majesty. Um." Shemal glanced at the other man at the table, who must be High Consort Allen. He was shockingly beautiful, his blond hair swept up in an elegant arrangement of braids and twists, decorated with jeweled birds and flowers. He smiled warmly, something about it relaxing Shemal. "I mean Your Majesties." He cleared his throat, then started his tale. "Several days ago, *late in the afternoon,* two men knocked *on my door. They said they had kidnapped Lord Bestowen* and needed me to watch him while they got their cart fixed. *So I sent them off, already planning to get Lord Bestowen home somehow. But when I removed the blanket covering him, I realized it was Commander Lesto.*"

"How did you know it was Commander Lesto?" the High Consort asked in a soft, pretty voice—and in perfect Islander. More than that, the High Consort spoke Shemal's dialect, from the island of Matarahira, what Mainlanders called the South Star Island. *"Have you encountered him before?"*

Shemal's cheeks went hot. *"Yes, when I was arrested some time ago for piracy. I did my pardon service, though, and have been reformed since."*

The High Consort smiled, turned to the High King, and repeated everything he'd said.

"He does what you do, with the back and forth that leaves the rest of us extremely confused," the High King said, looking at the High Consort with a fond smile.

"Lesto said that," Shemal said, then snapped his mouth shut, face burning hotter than ever. Mother Ocean drag him to the deep, he was not made for spending time around people like this.

The High King's head whipped back to him, brows shooting up. *"Lesto* said."

"I meant the High Commander—"

"Oh, no," the High King said, eyes gleaming. "You gave it away a little bit earlier, when I said you were Lesto's pirate. I know that look." He stood up, prowled close, green eyes intent and way more aware and knowing than Shemal liked. "Met him some time ago when you were arrested for piracy. Saved him from kidnappers instead of figuring out a way to earn money yourself. Risked your life to get him to safety, and you're wearing both of his rings which, until now, have never left his person."

"Sarrica—" the High Consort interjected, or tried to, but Sarrica carried on like he hadn't heard.

"So tell me pirate, are your intentions for my brother honest, or are you one more scheming bastard trying to use him?"

Shemal stared at him, eyes wide, heart thundering. "What are you talking about?"

"Don't try to lie to me!" Sarrica snapped and grabbed the front of his shirt. "It's obvious you've been fucking him. But I'm not going to let someone hurt Lesto again. So if you've managed to manipulate him and convince him that you care when you're just one more scheming bastard, if you've played him for a fool for his money and—"

Shemal didn't think, just reacted the way he always did when someone dared to insult and challenge him so. He might have been a pirate, a useless halfwit who could barely read and write and wasn't good for anything off a ship, but he wasn't the kind of bastard to lie or cheat a person, and he certainly wasn't the kind of bastard to play with someone's feelings.

So he swung, hard enough that Sarrica let him go and went stumbling back a step.

It was only as Sarrica gaped at him that Shemal realized what he'd just done. *"Oh, Mother Ocean."* He dropped to his knees and buried his face in his hands, not certain if he wanted to cry or throw up.

He'd just punched the High King of the Harken

Empire.

"Sarrica!" the High Consort snapped. "What in the name of the Pantheon were you thinking?"

"He's the one who hit *me*, you know," Sarrica said, and Shemal really had lost his mind because he sounded *amused* instead of angry.

"You deserved it! He was already terrified, and then you get in his face and threaten him like that—"

"He's almost bigger than me."

"He's also a former—" the High Consort slipped into Gaulden, then said something in Tricemorien, then Gearthish—then abruptly cut off.

Shemal looked up slowly, face going hot as he saw the reason for the abrupt silence: the High King was kissing his consort breathless.

Maybe he could sneak away and vanish into the city before they remembered he was there.

He'd just started to stand again when they drew apart.

"Don't try to sneak off," Sarrica said cheerfully. "We're not done with you. You're not going to be punished for hitting me, either. Not when everyone who knows me would just say I deserved it. Sit down before you pass out."

Shemal stared blankly. "What? I mean, Your Majesty?"

Sarrica lightly tested his jaw as he motioned to the table. "Sit. Down. Finish telling your story." The High Consort gave him a look, and Sarrica added, "I'm sorry for alarming you. Nice hit. I can see why Lesto likes you."

"Uh—" Shemal couldn't think of what to say.

Laughing again, Sarrica grabbed his arm and dragged him over to the table, pushed him into a chair that left Shemal with his back to the door. "Speaking of Lesto, you would probably like to know I received word he is doing well. Already walking about terrorizing his soldiers despite the healer begging him to stay abed."

"But he needed stitches," Shemal snapped. "On his left side and his right thigh, never mind he was poisoned! He shouldn't be walking around yet."

"Oh, I like you," Sarrica said and pushed a platter of bread, cheese, and olives toward him as well as a cup and a pitcher of dark, spiced wine. "Eat, drink. Tell us the rest of your story so I know how many heads need to roll."

Ignoring the food and drink, no matter how much his stomach growled, Shemal told them the rest of it. Leaving out, of course, the more personal interactions. From Sarrica's narrowed eyes, he wasn't fooling anyone with the omissions.

When he was finished, his voice had gone faintly hoarse.

"Drink," the High Consort said and pushed the cup and pitcher closer. "Please."

Shemal nodded stiffly and finally poured a cup of wine, some of his tension easing to have something wet on his throat and anything at all in his stomach. Four hard days of traveling practically nonstop had left him ready to eat a whale and sleep for a month. "I— I'm sorry he was hurt. I tried—"

"I've every faith you did your best, but ten against two is not odds I would enjoy." Sarrica smiled wryly. "Though I might have bragged about being more than capable of beating them as a youth. From what I've heard, you are the reason he's alive and safe." He slapped the table. "Once I've put the fear of the

Pantheon into Treya Mencee, we will head for Brimin and drag our good Commander home where he is certain to be safe until this matter is sorted." The High Consort rolled his eyes, and Sarrica scowled. "What?"

"It's just funny how alike the two of you are. You do something dangerous, he throws a fit about your reckless stupidity. He does something dangerous, you throw a fit about his rash behavior. You're like two sides of a mirror."

Sarrica grinned. "Now, now, High Consort, I think you are not fit to chide anyone for reckless behavior."

Allen's cheeks flushed. "I wasn't chiding, I was observing and mocking."

Laughing, Sarrica rose and stepped clear of the table, extended a hand that Allen took as he rose to his feet. "Shall we go have a proper meal and plot all the ways we are going to make Treya Mencee cry?"

"Yes," Allen said, the warmth of his eyes fading as anger overtook them, gave the jewel blue of them a storm cloud edge. He glanced at Shemal and the warmth returned. "If you'll follow us, one of the guards will escort you to your rooms. Eat, rest, and in the morning, you and Sarrica can leave for Brimin."

Shemal stood and obediently followed. Out in the hall, Allen spoke with the towering guard, who bowed and motioned for Shemal to follow him. They cut through several hallways, and more than a few soldiers stared at Shemal as he passed.

Was it always going to be like this if he was with Lesto? Staring, gawking, whispering. On his fingers, Lesto's rings weighed heavily and seemed to burn.

It was a relief when he was finally ushered through another set of double doors, into a large, handsome room. A meal had been set out on the table off to one side, the smells wafting from it making his stomach growl all over again.

But it looked like an awfully nice room for a pirate. He turned to the guard. "Are you sure this is my room?"

The guard shrugged. "Commander Lesto's room, which amounts to the same thing, right?" He flashed a quick grin. "So there's a rumor about you going 'round the garrison, bit of a wager, too."

Shemal felt faint. "Oh, no."

"Some are saying you're the fella what punched the Commander last year. They said those tattoos of yours are pretty memorable. Was that you?"

Shemal couldn't *breathe.* Was there any point in denying it? By the look of the guard's grin, there really wasn't. "If I say yes, will you promise not to tell His Majesty? And don't tell Lesto I told you."

The guard threw his head back and laughed. "Oh, Pantheon." He clapped Shemal on the back. "Wait until I tell everyone. They're going to lose it." He laughed a few seconds more, then straightened and tried to return to his serious demeanor. "If there's anything you need, there will be a guard stationed outside at all times. All you have to do is ask and the matter will be taken care of. We'll come wake you tomorrow. There should be clothes in the wardrobe. If none of them fit, just let us know. I hope you have a good night. If you want company, there are always people in the great hall, and they'd all love to talk to you." He flashed a last grin, then bowed and departed.

Well, that was new. Shemal wasn't certain he liked being bowed to. On the other hand, it was a vast improvement on being arrested.

He looked around the room again. There was the

table, a large, stately four poster bed with dark blue drapes that had been tied back. A matching duvet covered the bed itself. There was also a large wardrobe, two chests, and a stand meant to hold armor.

Near the table was a fireplace and a tub full of steaming water with a basket containing soap, rags, and other wash items nearby.

Being treated like he was important was more than a little strange, but he wasn't going to complain. Left to his own devices, he might have been able to scrounge up enough coin to rent a room in a vermin-infested hostel for the night, and his bath would have been a wash down with water he hauled from a public fountain with whatever he could borrow to carry it.

Stripping off his grimy clothes, he climbed into the tub and happily scrubbed himself clean. When he was done, however, he belatedly realized he needed a towel or—oh, there was a dressing robe hung by the fire. It was warm and soft as he pulled it on and belted it closed, and it seemed the epitome of luxury to sit and eat dinner wearing a dressing robe while still damp from his bath.

But all he could think about was the village where everything had gone wrong, the way he and Lesto had planned to enjoy the night before heading out in the morning. It had been a selfish, indulgent plan, but he wished it had happened. As it was, who knew what would happen next. What if Lesto changed his mind now that he was back where he belonged? What if the High King forbade the relationship and sent Shemal away? For all that Lesto seemed indifferent to Shemal's past, scores of others would not be so accepting. Lesto could do far better than a lowly pirate, and every single person in Harken probably wouldn't hesitate to remind him of that.

That was a problem for another day, though. For the present, his only dilemma was whether he should he start with the lamb, the fragrant rice, or the wine. He wished Lesto was there to share the meal with. For all he'd been looking forward to fucking Lesto when their meal was over, sitting and eating with him, talking and drawing out more of Lesto's smiles, had been more than enough.

Mother Ocean, he was not used to life moving quite so fast. It didn't seem like he should be hooked by someone so hard and fast, so immediately. But was it really immediate, given Lesto had been the driving force in his life the past year and a half? Shemal didn't know anymore. He just knew he missed Lesto and was worried about him. The fool should be resting, but Shemal had the feeling Lesto didn't rest unless he was tied down.

Smiling faintly at the thought, he finally filled his plate and began eating, moaning and marveling at the flavors, the skill with which everything had been cooked. Not the sort of fare he was used to, not by a league.

By the time he finally stopped, he was ready to pop. When was the last time he'd eaten so much? Probably the last time he'd slunk home to recuperate and add to his tattoos. Years, then.

After washing his face and hands, he doused all the lamps save one then crossed the room, stripped off his robe, and climbed into the enormous bed. It was wickedly soft; he was half afraid he'd go through it to the floor.

He lay back against the ridiculous pile of pillows,

exhausted but still wound too tightly to sleep. The remaining lamp light gleamed on his rings. He ran his thumb over the griffons of the High Crown, surrounded by starflowers and blood orchids.

But it was the other ring that really drew him. The bottom half he couldn't read; he recognized it was shorthand formal Harken but reading it was beyond his skills. He was more interested in the markings that formed the top half of the circle that surrounded the skull and swords. Those he could read, or should have been able to. They were sailing coordinates, but not quite right. They were, in fact, gibberish. Anyone who tried to use them to sail would wind up lost or dead, assuming they even managed to make sense enough to sail at all.

Lesto was going to tell him the secret of the coordinates. Shemal didn't understand how, after a year and a half, they had moved so far so fast. Part of him wanted to run away, flee back to a life that made sense, even if his options then were piracy or goats.

Though he was still at a loss as to what he would do when they reached Harkenesten. But that storm was still far off on the horizon. He could focus on other matters for a little while longer.

Blowing out the lamp by the bed, he shoved most of the pillows off the bed, pulled the blankets up, and fell asleep smiling.

~~*

He jerked awake to the sound of someone pounding on the door, shoving the heavy mass of his hair from his face as he stared blearily at the guard at the foot of the bed. "What?"

The man grinned. "Breakfast is ready. We depart in an hour for Brimin. Your boots have been cleaned; they're waiting by the table. If you need anything else, sir, just let us know."

"Um." Before Shemal could formulate a better reply, the man was gone.

He climbed out of bed and went to the wardrobe, pulling out clothes that looked like they might actually fit him. They couldn't be Lesto's. He wasn't as big and broad as Shemal, more the tall, lanky sort. Well, whatever, they were clean and they fit—why was he puzzling over them?

As promised, someone had come while he slept and taken his boots off for cleaning. They hadn't looked that nice when he'd bought them used in a small shop at the ass end of Rilien. He pulled them on, then quickly ate a breakfast that was as wonderful as dinner had been.

When he was done with that, he bound his heavy hair loosely back, pulled a jacket from the wardrobe, and shrugged into it as he headed out.

The guard posted at his door, the same one who'd woken him, stopped him with a lifted hand. "Pardon, sir, I forgot to give this to you earlier." He held out a small leather coin purse that proved to be shockingly heavy. There must be at least twenty regals in it. "The rest of the party will meet you in the courtyard."

"Thank you," Shemal said and tucked the coins away, biting back questions about why he was being given money for no reason because no way was he giving them the chance to change their minds. "Uh. Where is the courtyard?"

Grinning, the guard motioned for him to follow. "I'll show you. Everyone is in quite the tizzy over you.

The last time the Commander had a lover, it was some snotty jackass who was all sweetness and sunshine in front of the Commander and then turned into an evil little gremlin lord the moment he was out of sight."

"Uh—" Shemal floundered. "Did he live after Lesto found out?"

"Barely. I hear he hasn't left Delfaste since he ran home for protection." The guard looked over his shoulder. "Did you really punch him?"

Shemal made a face. "Yes, and I'm regretting it more and more. I can't be the only person who's punched Lesto and lived."

"His Majesty is the only other one that I've heard about," the guard replied. "Those two hit and shove each other all the time."

That surprised Shemal not a bit. The way they talked about each other, it was clear they were as tight as brothers. If it wasn't so obvious Sarrica was smitten with his consort, Shemal might have been afraid. Well, *more* afraid.

His thoughts skittered away as they reached the courtyard and he was immediately distracted by the sight of Lesto—rather, someone who looked a lot like Lesto, though on closer look, he was prettier, younger, not nearly as interesting. There was also the fact he had both eyes. He was speaking with the same young woman who'd been standing guard outside the High King's office the previous day. They looked up at the sound of footsteps, and the man's smile was very much like Lesto's. "Good morning. You must be the pirate I've heard so much about. I'm sorry we didn't meet last night; I was out with the guards rounding up Treya Mencee officials here in the city to see what information might be gleaned."

"Learn anything?"

"Maybe," the man said with a shrug. "The guards are still talking to them, but they'll send word to Brimin if they learn anything. It's the ones back at Harkenesten that will more likely be of use, and by now, they should have all been arrested." He extended a hand. "Rene Arseni. You can call me Rene." He shook Shemal's hand, but there was a stiffness to the movement. "This is Jac Denali, bodyguard to High Consort Allen."

"Shemal shey Variago. An honor to meet you."

"And you," Jac said with a grin. "So you punched the High Commander *and* the High King. Impressive." She winked when he groaned. "I'd better go, I'll see you later, Lord Rene."

Ren lifted a hand in farewell, and Shemal looked more closely at it. "You broke your hand."

Rene grimaced. "Yes, last year when a mission in Cartha went poorly. I'm lucky it works at all." He motioned to the waiting horses, falling into step alongside Shemal as they went to join the others. "So it is true you're the very same pirate who punched him?"

"I'm never going to hear the end of that, am I?" Shemal asked.

"No, probably not," Rene said with a laugh. "However, it's Lesto everyone will enjoy teasing relentlessly. He doesn't normally make it this easy for us to poke fun at him." He grinned again and turned to the others. "Good Morning, Your Majesties."

"It will be merrier when I am back in my own bed," Sarrica groused as he swung up into the saddle. "Move your ass, let's get this over with."

Allen rolled his eyes as he swung up into his own

horse, and smiled at Jac as she rode up to settle at his side. He moved closer to Sarrica, leaned over to kiss him softly. "Try to behave. I'll see you back home in a couple of weeks."

Sarrica grunted and stole a longer kiss before letting him go. He cast a glare toward the gathered guards who seemed to be serving as Allen's escort. When he was satisfied his glare had done whatever he wanted, he turned back to Rene and Shemal. "Mount up, let's go." After Shemal had mounted the horse a guard brought to him, Sarrica smirked and said, "So the guards have been telling me stories."

Shemal groaned again and buried his face in his hands. "That wasn't the deal."

"I'm the High King. Who did you think they were going to obey in the end? I can't wait to see Lesto. He's had this coming for a long time." Before Shemal could reply, he turned to the guards that had mounted up and gathered around them. "Are we ready?"

"Ready, Your Majesty."

"Then move out!"

A chorus of 'Yes, Majesty' filled the courtyard, and then they were racing out of the garrison and through the city, finally headed back to Lesto.

CHAPTER FIVE

"I'm going to fucking kill you!" Lesto bellowed, storming across the courtyard, armor and sword belt jangling.

Sarrica laughed. "It's good to see your health is improving."

Lesto gave him a hard shove. "Laugh one more time and see what happens to you. What in the fucking Realms are you doing here, you useless excuse for a High King? How many times do I have to tell you to stay where you're safe?" Sarrica opened his mouth, but Lesto whipped around to face Rene and kept going. "And you! When I'm not around, it's your job to keep him from being this stupid!"

"Even you can't keep him from being stupid on a good day," Rene replied. "I don't know why you expect me to do any better."

Lesto's expression darkened further as he took a step closer—and was reeled back by Sarrica.

"Calm down, Commander," Sarrica said, still grinning. "Honestly, you should be pleased that Allen didn't come this far. Once we knew you were well, he headed home. Well, he left the following morning, strictly speaking, but he did promptly volunteer—"

"Why did he come at all?!" Lesto said, knocking Sarrica's arm away and shoving him again. "Sarrica, I'm going to knock every last one of your teeth out!"

Sarrica lifted his hands to placate. "If it makes you feel any better, your lover already punched me."

"I don't care who—" Lesto stopped, jaw dropping. "What?"

Grin returning, Sarrica turned around, reached out, and dragged someone into their little circle.

The knot of fear that had settled in Lesto's chest began to loosen and unwind as he stared at Shemal. Then Sarrica's words came back to him. "You punched Sarrica?"

Shemal looked like he was going to be sick. "I didn't mean to."

Lesto rounded on Sarrica again. "What did you do?"

"You are in exceptional form today," Rene groused. "When are the healers going to listen to my advice and tie you down?"

"Be quiet unless you want to be knocked unconscious for a week," Lesto snapped, then turned back to Sarrica. "What did you do to him?"

Sarrica huffed. "I was making certain his intentions were honorable—"

Lesto punched him, sending Sarrica stumbling back a couple of steps. "I hope you meant that as a poor attempt at a joke."

"I'm being perfectly serious. I have a right to look after my brother," Sarrica said, touching his fingertips to his bleeding, swollen lip. "There is a gross lack of respect for the High King around here."

Lesto tensed to punch him again. "If you want respect, stop being a reckless fool and an interfering little brat. I swear to the Pantheon—"

"You're bleeding!" Shemal stepped in close, one of his hands going to Lesto's shoulder, the other to his side, where, sure enough, it looked like Lesto had probably torn his stitches. Again. Mishi was going to harangue him for hours if he found out. Damn it.

Lesto looked at Shemal, gently pulled away the hand on his side and held it fast, voice gruff as he said, "I'm fine. The stitches were supposed to be coming out soon anyway."

Shemal's frowned deepened. "If the wound was healed enough for them to come out, you wouldn't be bleeding like this."

"I'm fine, I promise," Lesto said.

"Oh, my gods," Sarrica and Rene said together.

Ire returning at the reminder of their presence, Lesto turned back and glared at them as nastily as he knew how. "If you think I'm done trying to beat sense into you halfwits, you are painfully mistaken."

"You *melted*," Rene said, still gaping. "He touched you, and you melted like *butter.* I didn't know you could *do* that."

Lesto stepped toward him, hands curling into fists.

Rene just broke into a grin. "You really are smitten, I can't believe it. With a pirate. Of *course* you are. It's *you.*"

"Shut up," Lesto snapped. "If you know what's good for you, you'll stay out of my sight the rest of the day." He gave Rene a rough shove then whipped around to Sarrica and jabbed him hard in the chest. "You had better be ready to return home in the morning."

Sarrica grabbed hold of him. "Are you going to stop being mad long enough for us to say we're happy you're alive and safe? You do remember you were kidnapped and we've been worried about you, right?"

Shoulders slumping as his anger faded, Lesto gave a jerky nod. "If you were so damned worried about me, you halfwit, you should have stayed where you were safe so we didn't have to worry about you coming to harm as well."

"Shut up," Sarrica said and hugged him tightly. Lesto returned it, finally letting relief wash through him.

Letting go of Sarrica, he turned to hug Rene. "I'm sorry I worried you."

Rene chuckled as he drew back. "We were more worried about how much destruction you would cause. Of all the people to get kidnapped."

"Stop talking," Lesto said gruffly and pushed him away. "Get out of my sight before I remember how much I still want to punch you." He jabbed Sarrica's chest. "I wasn't kidding about going home tomorrow. See that you're ready to leave at first light." He turned away before Sarrica could reply, taking hold of Shemal's hand again as he walked off.

Shemal pulled his hand free a few steps later. "Are you all right?"

"I'm fine, just surrounded by halfwits and tired of being wounded," Lesto said with a sigh, some of his tension bleeding away. "Are you all right? I know you must be exhausted after saving me and then heading almost immediately back out..." He looked up at Shemal, steps slowing until they stopped in the middle of the long hall they were in.

Shemal smiled, a little sweet, a little impish. "I'm fine. They even let me sleep in the High Commander's bed last night. Wish I had a bed like that every night."

"You will," Lesto said, a hint of growl in his voice. He pushed until Shemal was against the wall then leaned in and kissed him hard, hungry and impatient, needing to feel and taste for himself that all was well again. That Shemal still wanted him even after all the days they'd been apart, all the trouble that Lesto had already proven to be.

That he would always be, because of his proximity to the High King. Sarrica was a flame, and those who stood too close learned to live with the heat, ran away, or were destroyed by it.

Shemal made a soft noise against his mouth, and then his hands, warm and heavy and calloused, framed Lesto's face as the kiss slowly eased, turning soft and lingering. The finest tremor ran through his body as Lesto's fingers skated down his side.

Drawing back, Lesto stared into those too-pretty eyes. "I'm sorry, this is all probably way more hassle than you wanted. As much as I hated it when I thought you'd run away, I never really blamed you for that decision. You're not the first to make it."

"Nobles are a bunch of soft, whiny children," Shemal said, mouth ticking up in a small grin. "Mainlanders in general are useless. So it's not like any of this ruckus is a *surprise*."

Lesto jabbed him in the gut. *Hard.* "You're one to talk of ruckus. First you punched me, then you punched the High King? I can't tell if you're brave, mad, or trying to die."

"Can we please not talk about me punching the High King?" Shemal replied, eyes pinching shut. "I didn't mean to, it just happened. I didn't like his implication that I was lying to you, using you. Like I would even know what to do with a duchy or whatever."

"We're all overprotective of each other," Lesto said, reluctantly pulling away. "If Allen had appeared out of nowhere instead of being meticulously selected, I'd have asked the same questions—and probably been a lot meaner about it."

Shemal laughed. "Yes, I can see why so many people go running when they hear your name. The man who picks a fight with the High King on a daily basis has little reason to fear the rest of the world, which would make you positively terrifying to most. That's part of the reason I punched you. When you walked out of the palace that day we met, you had everyone enthralled. They were scared but also adoring. I wanted to see what would happen if I hit you."

"Did you get what you expected?" Lesto asked, though he wasn't at all certain he wanted to know the answer. Obviously his reaction hadn't driven Shemal away, but...

Shemal smiled, all mischief and secrets. "No. You've never been what I expected." He leaned forward and dragged his mouth across Lesto's, leaving a trail of fire and sending a hot rush down Lesto's spine. "I like the unexpected." He drew back, licked his lips. "It's more attractive than it should be that you're not afraid of anything."

"I'm afraid of plenty," Lesto said as they resumed walking again. "I was afraid you might not come back, for one."

"I promised—"

"That wasn't it," Lesto cut in hastily, stopping them again. "Like I said, my life is a bit much for anyone to put up with." He stared into Shemal's eyes, drunk on just how fucking pretty they were, all the life that filled them. "You'd be surprised how many people decided that even an annual income of forty thousand crowns wasn't worth the trouble."

Shemal's eyes widened, and for a moment, he

looked like he couldn't breathe. "Forty—" He choked, coughed. "That's a lot of fucking money."

Lesto burst out laughing—and laughed harder when Shemal scowled at him. Bright, sharp affection rushed through him, and he was helpless against tugging Shemal in for another kiss.

The sound of noise at the end of the hall startled them apart, and Lesto motioned for Shemal to follow him, heading down the hall and through an archway to the backstairs. On the second floor, he cut right and headed down the hall to his room.

When the door was closed and locked behind them, Lesto removed his armor and set it on its stand, put his sword belt on the trunk next to it, then sat on the bed to get rid of his boots before stripping off his under tunic.

"Should I get the healer?" Shemal asked, then made a face. "Not that I know where to find them."

"I'm sure someone has already ratted me out," Lesto replied, then smiled faintly. "That's why I locked the door."

Shemal didn't return the smile, too intent on frowning at Lesto's bleeding side. Really, though, the bleeding had practically stopped. He'd just overworked the last little stubborn bit high on his ribs that wasn't healing as quickly as the rest. "You're hurt."

"I've seen scars on you that are worse than anything I've got," Lesto said, moving over to the table where Mishi had left supplies for him with a long-suffering sigh after Lesto had hurt himself the previous day clobbering a group of halfwit cadets. They were going to wind up on wall duty in Tricemore if they didn't pull their heads out of their asses. "I doubt you got proper treatment."

"Yeah, and the wounds lasted longer than they should have and hurt constantly, sometimes so badly I couldn't sleep for long, if at all, until they were half-healed. Ever been scratched by a thorn rat? That was days of white-hot agony I still remember ten years later. If we'd had a healer, they could have applied a poultice that would have eased the pain in a matter of hours. Instead, I suffered for almost two weeks."

Lesto sighed. "You make your point, but I promise, this particular tear isn't any major worry. I just need to clean and bandage it. Help if you want."

Shemal's frown eased slightly as he joined Lesto at the table and with quick, sure movements, removed the stitches, cleaned the wound, and covered it with a fresh bandage.

"I'm not sure why I'm surprised you're good at that. A skill born of necessity, like your silver tongue leanings?" Lesto smiled. "You have elegant hands."

"Elegant?" Shemal snorted and washed his hands in the bowel of water on the table, dried them with a rag from a stack. "I've been called a lot of things, but elegant is definitely new." He flexed his hands, calloused and scarred, the fingers long and deft. They weren't pretty hands, but neither were Lesto's. "I'm fairly certain elegant is not the word."

Lesto stepped in close, rested his hands on Shemal's hips, and leaned in to brush a kiss across his mouth. "It is most definitely the word. You're good with your hands, that lends elegance. Even if you're too good for my fancy words."

"Never said that," Shemal said with a faint grin and drew him into another kiss that banished Lesto's plans for the rest of the day with shocking ease. Let the garrison take care of itself, and the less he saw of those two halfwits he called family, the better for them.

He slid his hands around and down, digging his fingers into the fine ass he'd admired even when he'd been so exhausted he could barely see straight. Then, admiring was all he could do. Now, though, he could do a good deal more than—

"Oh, no," Shemal said, drawing back, stepping firmly out of reach. "That will make your injuries worse for certain."

Lesto glared. "I'm fine. Get back here. If I wanted lectures and fussing, I'd go find Mishi or Sarrica. I want *you.* Without having to rush or be furtive."

Shemal glared right back. "Yes, and if I was the one with those injuries, you'd be the one saying it's not happening. You're definitely one of those rock-headed halfwits who gets mad when everyone else ignores their injuries and hurts, but will walk around with a broken leg and say you're fine. The sort of fusspot hypocrite that drives the rest of us mad. Do you know how many sailors die because of nonsense like that?"

"Did you just call me a *fusspot*?" Lesto demanded.

Folding his arms across his chest, Shemal replied, "Yes, because it's *true.* Tell me that anything I've said is wrong."

Lesto opened his mouth, closed it, then muttered, "I'm not a fusspot."

Shemal's glare turned into a crooked grin. "Yes, you are. One of the volatile ones, like my mother. You could tell when she was really worried about you because she'd haul off and backhand you hard enough you'd wake up on the other side of the island." A surprised laugh got the better of Lesto, and Shemal's grin widened. "You'd probably like my mother, come to think of it."

"I'm High Commander of the Imperial Army," Lesto said, turning stiffly away and heading for the wardrobe. "If I took proper care of every little injury I acquired, I'd spend all my time in bed instead of getting things done. I'd look weak and incapable, and there's also the fact that halfwits like Sarrica never fucking listen to me. So I'm sorry I'm a damned fusspot hypocrite, but I have a job to do."

That he should probably get back to since all his stupid hopes for being selfishly indulgent for once in his life obviously weren't going to happen.

He yanked the wardrobe open and found a clean undertunic, threw it toward the bed, and turned back for a tunic. Snatching one off the shelf, he whipped around—

—and barely stopped in time to avoid slamming into Shemal. "What? I can get dressed on my own, you know."

"At no point since the first time I saw you have I ever had a single thought about getting your clothes *on,*" Shemal replied.

Lesto wanted to stay mad, but he was helpless against the smile that overtook his face. "Well, that makes good hearing, at least. But I've been rather firmly told that the rest of them will not be coming off, so move out of my way so I can dress."

"I didn't mean to hurt you," Shemal said, "but I am fairly certain that if you're going to worry about me, which I know you have, then you have to accept that I worry about you, too. I've always made a point of avoiding, uh, this kind of thing, but even I know a thing like worry goes both ways."

"This kind of thing," Lesto echoed, the last of his

anger fading. "I'm a fusspot and you're relationship shy. What a pair."

Shemal's cheeks flushed. "I'm not—" He broke off when Lesto snickered. "*Fine.* Fair enough." He reached out and pulled the tunic from Lesto's hand, threw it aside then pulled him in and kissed him. With intent. No mistaking a kiss like that.

Lesto drew back only when he needed desperately to draw a proper breath. "I distinctly remember someone telling me this wouldn't be happening."

"Well, we're certainly not reliving what we did the first time," Shemal replied, walking backward toward the bed and dragging Lesto with him. "My knees were bruised for days, and the rest of me wasn't much better off."

"You should have seen the places *I* had bruises," Lesto groused, though he hadn't regretted them until Shemal had abruptly abandoned him, left him feeling used and foolish.

Shemal sat on the bed, drew Lesto between his thighs, and dragged that hot, distracting mouth across his throat, lingering where his pulse beat to suck up a mark.

Lesto's breath hitched, fingers twitching before he rested his hands on Shemal's heavy thighs. Fuck, he hadn't forgotten the feel of them at all, even discounting the reminder in the bath. There weren't many people that could make him feel small, even though he wasn't actually big, just tall and often covered in armor and aggravation. Shemal, though, made him feel small, in a way he wasn't used to at all. "Is there any chance of convincing you to fuck me?"

"I think past precedent has established I'm not much good at resisting that particular request,"

Shemal said, throat working, eyes sliding shut. When he opened them again, they were dark and hot, pupils large enough to swallow much of the beautiful teal. "I don't think your wounds will thank me much."

"I really am better healed than any of you are crediting," Lesto said with a huff. "It's been more than a week. I have waited long enough to have you in my bed, pirate."

Shemal grinned, hot as a midday sun at the peak of summer. "Far be it for me to keep arguing, Commander." He dropped his hands to stroke and squeeze Lesto's trapped cock, leering slightly as he added, "I'm more than ready to get on with the *having.*"

Rolling his eye, Lesto stepped back and worked on getting his breeches off. "You're still wearing clothes."

"I guess it would be rude to keep them on at this point. Even an uncouth heathen like me knows that much," Shemal said, and with truly impressive speed, he sent his clothes to join Lesto's breeches on the floor. Getting hold of Lesto's arm, he dragged him onto the bed and pushed him into the bedding. "Now, then—"

They both went still when someone knocked on the door.

"Leave or I'll put you in stocks!" Lesto shouted.

There was one last, hard rap on the door, a *you'll definitely hear about this later* warning, and then whoever it was—Mishi, likely—departed.

Shemal laughed. "Subtle."

"I have never been accused of subtlety or patience," Lesto replied. "Those are not the skills I am paid to possess."

"Fair enough," Shemal said and bent to kiss him,

bracing his hands on either side of Lesto, leaning over him like a bank of storm clouds bent on soaking the entire continent.

Lesto was more than willing to let the storm have him. He rested his hands on that fine, warm skin, slid them back to dig his fingers into the lovely muscles of Shemal's back, keeping him close to better suck and lick and savor that irresistible mouth. He whined in protest when Shemal drew back. "What?"

"I thought it would be better to have something slick now, rather than have to stop to look for it later," Shemal said, then bent to lick across his lips before sucking on the bottom one, pulling away slowly with a drag of teeth that made Lesto shiver.

"There's a basket on the shelf under the table," Lesto said.

Shemal rolled away, that wicked little grin on his face, and knelt on the floor. Lesto could hear him rifling around in the basket for a moment before he found the little glass vial Lesto had put there the last time he'd been at that garrison. Mostly for self-gratification, but also the low-burning hope that eventually he might have company.

It was still hard to believe all that hoping had come to something.

Climbing back on the bed, Shemal spread Lesto's thighs, mindful of the injured one, and settled between them like he belonged there. Lesto certainly wasn't denying it. The problem with always being in charge was that people assumed he was in charge in *all* circumstances.

He'd tried to tell exactly one other lover what he'd wanted, and they'd laughed, thinking he was joking, and told him to stop delaying and get on with it. He hadn't felt comfortable telling any of the others, which he'd realized rather too late was a sign they weren't worthy lovers.

Only one person, other than Sarrica, had ever done what he asked without hesitation or question, hadn't seen it as strange.

Lesto curled a hand into Shemal's heavy hair and drew him down into a deep kiss, loving the way it already felt so familiar, so necessary. Drawing back, he said, "I've been waiting a long time, pirate. You better be at least as good as my memory."

Emotions too tangled to sort rippled across Shemal's face, and he gave Lesto a quick, hard kiss that lingered like spicy peppers before shifting to put that evil, highly memorable mouth to work elsewhere. His teeth nipped at soft skin, his tongue dragged over scars, though as focused as he clearly was on trying to make Lesto scream, Shemal never once forgot about Lesto's wounds.

By the time he lapped at the wet smears left on Lesto's skin by his aching, eager cock, Lesto was desperate enough to kill him, except then the lovely torment would cease. "Are you going to let me touch you?"

"Not while you're injured," Shemal said, looking up the length of Lesto's body through his long lashes. "Hold still and do as you're told, Commander."

Lesto groaned, liking that more than he would ever admit, though the way his cock twitched, he didn't *have* to say. Shemal chuckled, low and addictive, and finally dropped that distracting mouth of his over Lesto's cock, sucking with expertise, throat tight and hot, tongue more flexible than a tongue had any right to be. Lesto shuddered hard, dropping one hand to fist in that thick, heavy mass of hair, his other hand tangling in the blanket as he thrust deeper into Shemal's throat.

Shemal took it with ease, sucking harder, working Lesto's cock until it was impossible to hold back. Lesto came with a ragged cry he didn't bother to muffle. It was his room and his garrison and he seldom got to enjoy anything but his own hand. That was more than enough for some people, but Lesto had never been one of them.

Drawing back, Shemal wiped spit and come from his lips and chin with the back of his hand. Sweat gleamed on his tattooed skin. Fuck if that wasn't the most erotic image Lesto had ever seen. Lesto leaned up enough to grab hold of his shoulders and dragged him into a wet, messy kiss. Shemal groaned into his mouth, pushed him down into the bedding with all that lovely weight, and rutted jerkily against him.

He spilled just moments later, still kissing Lesto, feeding every moan and garbled word into his mouth. When he eventually went still, they both were panting softly, the only sound in the room, the noise of the garrison a distant, negligible murmur.

"You were supposed to fuck me," Lesto said eventually. "I suppose I can forgive you since it means you have to stay here until you get around to it."

Shemal laughed and rolled off him, went to the table to wet a cloth that he brought back to clean them both. He tossed it to join their discarded clothes when he was done then stretched out beside Lesto, a long, loose-limbed, half-wild beauty too breathtaking to be settling for the difficult life of lover to the Duke of Fathoms Deep.

Lesto reached out and stroked his fingers over the

rings Shemal still wore.

"Oh, right, I should return these," Shemal said and pulled the rings from his finger before Lesto could say he hadn't particularly minded. He liked seeing his ring on Shemal's finger. It was true he needed the imperial ring back, but he wouldn't be needing it for much longer. He hadn't missed its presence in the slightest, and realizing that would have set his mind on retirement if he hadn't already come to that decision.

He slid the rings on his own fingers, too sated and lazy to bother getting up for something as trivial as a chain.

Shemal caught his hand as he lowered it, ran his thumb over the rings much as Lesto had a moment ago. "Are you going to be missed, staying in here?"

"They're happiest when I'm out of sight and mind, and I almost never visit this garrison anymore, anyway," Lesto said with a snort. "Even if they did need me, they'd have to manage without. Everyone with half a brain knows exactly why I locked the two of us in here and just how painfully they'll die if they interrupt us for any reason."

"I see," Shemal said with a laugh. He pressed his face against Lesto's shoulder, and Lesto could feel the soft, warm brush of his lips. "What about the mercenaries? The kidnappers?"

"The kidnappers are long gone, and I think it safe to say whatever is going on, it comes back to Treya Mencee and Lord Bestowen. By now, Sarrica has ordered everyone even remotely connected to those two groups arrested or otherwise held until he sees fit to deal with them. Anyone not already at Harkenesten is currently being dragged there one way or another. So there is nothing for us to do until we're home again."

"So it would not be completely remiss of me to take a nap and then wake up to fulfill a promise to fuck you?"

Lesto smiled, lifted a hand to curl it into Shemal's hair. "You'd be remiss not to do precisely those things. I can't remember the last time I took a nap. I certainly have never dropped everything to spend time with a lover. I'm sure that rightfully upset most of them."

"Who cares about the previous ones?" Shemal asked with a smile. "I think we both know what I'll do if you ever stop paying sufficient attention to me."

"Yes, I can guess," Lesto said. "Your ability and willingness to throw a punch is certainly a testament to your belonging here."

That got him a smile worth all the gold in Harken, and a kiss that banished any last ingrained desire to get back to work.

He settled more comfortably and fell into a doze, enjoying the distant, muted thrum of the garrison, the much closer sounds of Shemal's steady breathing beside him, the warmth and weight draped along his side.

At some point, he stirred to the sound of the door unlocking, but Rene and Sarrica were the only other two who possessed a key to his room, so Lesto didn't bother moving. There was more noise, and the smell of food stirred him faintly, but then it all faded off again, and he happily let sleep pull him back under.

When he stirred the second time, it was to deft fingers wrapped around his cock and a tongue dragging across one nipple.

"Shemal..."

Looking up, Shemal said, "I like when you say my

name that way, all rough and needy, too sleepy to do anything but what you want."

"What I want is for you to get back to work," Lesto said and growled several choice words when Shemal instead withdrew.

He was somewhat mollified when he realized it was only so Shemal could slick his fingers. Lesto spread his legs gladly, reaching back to grab tightly to the bedding on either side of his head.

"This is much more fun when we're not in a hurry," Shemal murmured against his mouth before kissing him, tasting like wine and candied fruit. Someone had gotten up to enjoy a snack, and leave it to Sarrica to dig up something as hard to find in Brimin as candied fruit.

A slick finger pushed at Lesto's hole, teasing and gently pushing, pressing in so slowly Lesto could think of nothing else, could only suck and lick greedily at Shemal's mouth as he worked Lesto open.

By the time he'd gotten two fingers inside, twisting and stretching, hitting that spot and making Lesto howl, he was ready to fall apart.

Drawing back with a last kiss, Shemal slicked his cock and slowly pushed into Lesto's body. "Much, much better when I'm not as frantic as a *gishti* and still have a prison chain dangling from one ankle. Although I wouldn't mind fucking you that hard again once your leg can handle it. Bend you over a table, maybe, instead of spreading you out on the floor."

Lesto bucked his hips, took Shemal's cock deep, winning a startled a groan and a full body shudder. "Less talking, more fucking. I thought you pirates were all about action, not discussion."

Those teal eyes flashed, and Shemal wrapped his

hands tightly around Lesto's hips. "You want action, Commander?" He drew back and then slammed in hard, huffing a ragged laugh when Lesto groaned. Did it again, then even faster after that, leaving Lesto overwhelmed by sensation and the force of his thrusts, helpless to do anything but tighten his hold on the bedding and submit to the pounding.

He screamed Shemal's name when he came only a short time later, was still coming down from the release when he felt Shemal's last few short, jerking thrusts before Shemal plastered to him and shuddered through his climax.

Lesto was almost ready to go right back to sleep, but the growling of his stomach was more distracting than his lethargy. When he could breathe properly again, he nudged at Shemal to get off him, then slowly sat up and slid from the bed on stiff, still faintly wobbly limbs. "Hungry? Though I suspect you already had a snack."

Shemal's cheeks flushed. "Only wine and some of the *chilri-takata*. I've never seen so much of it in one place. I almost ate all of it."

"Well, you certainly *can* eat all of it," Lesto said. "I like it, but I don't love it. Tins of candied fruit are considered a romantic gift; Sarrica probably thought he was being clever." He walked over to the table and saw the candied fruit wasn't the only effort Sarrica had made—Lesto knew for a fact his favorite wine wasn't stored anywhere on the premises, and the garrison definitely didn't cook lamb that well.

Far be it for him to complain about the perks of being the best friend of the High King.

He sat down and poured a cup of wine, then piled his plate with food. Shemal dragged the chair on the opposite end of the table over to sit close to Lesto. "This looks amazing. I'm going to be become fat and spoiled eating food like this all the time." His expression said he still couldn't believe it was a possibility.

Whatever it took, Lesto would ensure that expression was wiped away completely. He might be a fool moving too quickly, but not a single slow, careful, considered relationship had ever made him burn. The day they'd met, he and Shemal hadn't even really talked. Lesto hadn't even known his name, and their frantic encounter had lasted only minutes. But he hadn't forgotten a single scrap of those stolen moments. He'd remembered every second for a year and a half.

He'd lived long enough to know that meant something.

CHAPTER SIX

Shemal opened his eyes then promptly closed them again. Tried to focus on his breathing until the panic subsided.

All for nothing since it just came rushing back when he opened his eyes again and stared around the simple but opulent bed chamber. He hadn't paid much attention the previous night, more interested in falling asleep than anything else, and the palace as a whole had been distracting enough.

Today, alone in the middle of a bed bigger than some rooms he'd lived in, sprawled on a soft down mattress piled with silk and linen, it was hard not to feel like an interloper who was going to get caught any moment and thrown into the first empty dungeon cell.

Lesto was gone, but Shemal vaguely remembered a soft kiss and a murmur that he had to go, that Shemal should go back to sleep.

A pity that. Everything would be a good deal less overwhelming with Lesto present. He also wouldn't have minded waking Lesto up with a hard fuck.

Shemal was, at least in theory, an adult though. He'd manage just fine on his own, same as he always had. Probably. Shemal gave it three hours before he mortally offended someone. Hopefully, whatever he did, it wouldn't hurt Lesto.

Drawing a deep breath, Shemal let it out slowly, threw back the blankets, and slid out of bed.

A dressing robe was draped over the foot of the

bed, and he assumed it was meant for him, given that another was hanging on a nearby hook, the armor stand next to it empty.

He shrugged into it and belted it closed as he slowly ventured out of the bedchamber and into the main room of the suite. There were two other doors, but Shemal couldn't remember what they were. Seeing no one around, and having nothing else to do, he tried both.

The first was another bedroom, free of dust but dark and bare of even sheets on the bed. It was somehow sad, but on the other hand, he didn't see the point in having his own bed when he could use the one that had Lesto in it.

The second door proved to be locked. Maybe an office or storage or something.

Which left him with nothing to do and nowhere to go. Food would be a good start, but he had no idea how to go about getting that.

Staying in Lesto's rooms in a dressing robe certainly wouldn't get him very far. Returning to the bedroom, he found a bowl and pitcher of water with a dish of soap nearby. Washed up, he ventured through a door that led to a dressing room, as anticipated.

And there was a pile of clothes and a note with his name on it. He could read that much Harken without problem, thankfully. Hopefully nobody would expect him to read more anytime soon.

He wasn't remotely surprised the clothes fit him almost perfectly, though he wished they weren't so fancy. He was used to homespun. The most expensive things he paid for were good boots and a warm coat.

In the end, he couldn't quite bring himself to wear all of it. He felt like he was putting on airs, pretending to be something he wasn't. The shirt and the breeches he kept, as well as the stockings and slightly too big shoes. But the ornate jacket with gold and pearl buttons, no matter how beautiful, was too much. Instead, he poked around the dressing room a bit and found a long, colorful silk and velvet wrap that he folded over twice and wore as a sash around his waist, tucking the ends into the small of his back. Hopefully Lesto wouldn't mind the borrowed wrap.

Pity he couldn't borrow some of Lesto's jewelry. He had some stunning pieces. The earrings were Shemal's favorite, from simple jewel studs to hoops and other dangling earrings of such beauty he would give anything to wear a pair for just an hour. They were far beyond Shemal's shamefully cheap, plain hoops. Did Lesto ever wear any of his jewelry? He'd only ever seen Lesto the soldier and Lesto the bedraggled hostage. Well, there was also Lesto the well-fucked. Heat curled lazily through him at the idea of Lesto in glittering jewelry and very little else. Teal was Lesto's official color, and he wore it well, but with that complexion and his gray eye... Shemal would give a lot to see him in black pearls and blood-red rubies.

Tucking those lovely thoughts away to savor later, Shemal finally left the dressing room—just as he heard the main door open and close, footsteps striding briskly toward the bedroom. Not Lesto's stride, unfortunately. Not hard enough, and it didn't jangle.

A tall, handsome woman stopped in the open doorway, sharp brown eyes sweeping the room. She startled slightly when she actually saw him then broke into a smile. "Good afternoon, my lord."

Shemal laughed. "I'm no lord."

Her smiled widened, turned a bit mischievous.

MEGAN DERR

"Not yet, but the palace is already buzzing about the man Commander Lesto brought home and dragged into his private chambers. Everybody thought he'd be accepting an offer from Ketherow or making one to Norring now that—" She broke off, shook her head. "My apologies, I'm starting in the middle rather than at the beginning." Stepping further into the room, she sketched a small bow, head dipping gracefully. Her hair was dark brown, but lighter than her skin, and flared out around her head. Freckles dusted her broad nose and cheeks. "My name is Bani Hashita, I am one of Lord Lesto's private secretaries. He's bid me show you around and assist you howsoever you need as you acclimate to palace life." She frowned slightly. "Were the clothes not adequate? Was there something wrong with the jacket?"

"No, the jacket was lovely. I just don't care to be weighed down by so much fabric," Shemal said. "Uh, thank you. What do you mean private secretary?"

She smiled. "I help in the handling of the Fathoms Deep Estate and related matters, rather than his military duties. He has four private secretaries and five military secretaries."

That was a lot of secretaries. "I hope I'm not causing you any problems."

She tilted her head slightly, regarded him pensively, and after a moment, that mischievous smile appeared again. Winking, she finally replied, "If you weren't here, my lord, I would be delivering papers to the tax office or getting different papers filed at the court. Believe me, you're doing me a favor."

Shemal laughed. "Well, I'm glad I'm proving useful. I don't suppose we could find food before doing anything else?"

"I can have lunch brought here, or we could go the public banquet hall," Bani replied. "Though if we go to the hall, you're in for a good deal of staring and whispering. Possibly some rude or hostile confrontations. More than a few are displeased by what your arrival, and obvious relationship with Lord Lesto, represents."

"I'm not going to begin my stay here by hiding," Shemal said with a shrug. "The confrontations will happen eventually. No point in delaying or prolonging the matter. It'll worsen with the waiting."

"As you wish." Bani smiled. "I can see why Lord Lesto likes you. This way, my lord, I'll show you some of the major parts of the palace along the way."

"Is there any point in telling you not to call me 'my lord'?" It had been strange enough when the soldiers called him 'master' and 'sir'.

"No, people made assumptions when they heard Lord Lesto had a new lover, and now they can't take it back without seeming rude. Lord Lesto also hasn't told anyone to stop, and no one is going to do anything that might possibly cross him. Many are already assuming it's only a matter of time before you'll require an honorific anyway."

Shemal surrendered with a sigh. He didn't know why they assumed it was just a matter of time before he became a lord. He wouldn't be a lord except by way of marriage, and that was an assumption even he did not have the nerve to make. Never mind that would be moving a bit fast.

"Any foods you're allergic to or detest? Drinks? Scents?" Bani asked as she led the way out of the suite and into a beautiful hallway.

Shemal vaguely remembered being told Lesto's

rooms were part of the imperial wing. He could see the ornate doors, complete with ominous guards, that must lead to the chambers of the High King and Consort down another hallway. "If I'm allergic to something, I've yet to encounter it. I'll eat anything put in front of me, though I'm happier when I don't have to eat fish."

"Really?" Bani's brows rose.

"It's disgraceful, I know, but I've never liked fish," Shemal said with a shrug. He loved his homeland, was proud to be an Islander, but there were too many things about life there that he didn't get along with for him to have ever been happy staying there. He and his family were content with the occasional visit—and they certainly didn't mind all the money he'd sent them over the years.

Bani scribbled something in the small leather-bound journal she'd pulled out of a pocket of her long, fancy-looking scarlet and purple jacket. "You're probably aware this is the imperial wing; access is restricted and rigidly enforced by Fathoms Deep. Sometimes you'll see the Three-headed Dragons instead, on the rare occasion Fathoms Deep is pulled away. The Dragons serve the High Consort, so you'll see them quite a bit in other places. Anyone else, be suspicious. Down that hall, you'll find your way to the public offices of the High King and Consort, Lord Lesto's military offices, other such things. You can get to the judiciary hall, the tax offices, and treasury, as well as a few other places down that hall, but there are shorter routes you'll learn eventually. Going *that* way will take you through some semi-private rooms, then on to the public rooms, eventually to private residence halls. And there are direct lines to the different sections of the palace from the compass hall. Now *this* hall is the fastest way to the banquet hall from here, though if you're downstairs, the rose garden is best."

Shemal tried to tuck all the information away, but he resigned himself to getting lost at least half a dozen times a day for as long as he was allowed to be there. He'd gawked at the size of the imperial palace on the rare occasions he saw it, had been dumbfounded when he'd been dragged into the pavilion because seeing it from a distance did it no justice. There were no words to describe the mass and majesty of it inside.

He understood less and less what Lesto, surrounded by all this beauty and splendor, found appealing in a scruffy pirate with no manners and poor survival instincts.

By the time they made it to the banquet hall, his head was spinning with information. Every last bit of it fled as a silence fell like a wave lapping at the shore, the chatter returning only as he passed every table until Bani led him up the stairs to the table that was obviously where the imperial family and their guests sat. "I don't think I'm supposed to be up here."

"High Consort Allen added your name to the list this morning," Bani said. "If I sat you anywhere else, I'd get my ears blistered and punished with a refresher class in High Court etiquette."

"There are *classes* for that?" Shemal hoped he didn't sound as terrified as he felt.

Bani ducked her head as she burst into giggles, but before Shemal could say anything else, a servant came up with two plates of food, another behind him bearing cups and two pitchers. "We have spiced cider and a golden Hemeria."

Hemeria—that was a word Shemal actually knew.

The captain of a ship he'd worked for three years had been obsessed with wine. They'd nearly wound up fish food because the damned man was determined to capture a Tricemorien galleon carrying barrels of Hemerian wine—and about two hundred Penance Gate mercenaries lent out by the High Crown to deal with troublesome pirates.

"The cider," he replied, because he'd drunk an entire cup of Hemerian wine, and the only thing he'd learned was that it wasn't worth getting stabbed and thrown overboard.

He could feel hundreds of eyes on him as he watched. "You weren't exaggerating about the attention I was going to draw. Are they always going to stare at me?"

"The short answer is yes, and you should probably hear the long answer if you want to survive."

"Why do I feel that being a pirate was less hazardous?" Shemal muttered, making her laugh again. He took a long swallow of cider, which was the best he'd ever tasted, and said, "Let's have it."

"Over to your left, gold hair and wearing a bright green jacket," Bani replied, and waited until Shemal had skimmed casually over the room and noted him before continuing. "That is the Lord Tecilia Ketherow, second son of the Duke of Balon. He has long been favored as an ideal match for Lord Lesto. Their estates are in close proximity, both deal heavily in wheat, both are old, wealthy, and powerful titles. Lord Tecilia bought a brewery some time ago and is considered an expert in beer, which would match nicely with the movements into beer that Fathoms Deep has recently begun. He also has a brother in the navy."

"Admiral Ketherow," Shemal said. That was why

the name sounded familiar. "He's talked about often as a man to be avoided."

Bani nodded. "That's the one. Lord Tecilia has been the favorite for years, even though any of us who know Lord Lesto could tell you it would never happen. I think people assume that His Majesty will eventually arrange a marriage or force Lesto to finally pick someone." She laughed as Shemal snorted. "Yes, exactly. Lord Lesto manages His Majesty, and in return His Majesty is smart enough not to try and manage Lord Lesto."

Shemal gave Lord Tecilia a longer look, not particularly concerned about being caught staring as the man kept staring openly at him. He was handsome, tending toward pretty, but he also looked soft, all silk and lawn, skin a pale brown, his hair a fluffy golden cloud around his head. "Is he old enough to marry?"

"You sound like Lord Lesto," Bani replied with a small grin. "He's the popular choice at court, though, and the one likely to give you trouble. But some of the older crowd think Lesto will eventually approach Lord Kamir Norring, youngest son of the Viscount of Tesly."

Shemal dragged his eyes away from the gawkers, frowning. "Norring, that name sounds familiar."

"Possibly because they're an exceptionally wealthy family, and moderately powerful, even before they were granted the Tesly title a few generations ago. Tesly and Norring have long histories in Tricemore." Bani replied. "His brother is the heir and tends the family estate while the parents reside here in the palace. His sister is Captain of the Shadow Bell mercenaries."

Shemal's mouth tightened. *That* was why the name sounded familiar. Shadow Bell—all Islanders knew that damned name. Shadow Bell was an old mercenary band, and they believed in a lot of old ways, like conscripting dirty Islanders and putting them at the front lines so the superior Mainland soldiers were less likely to die. "So they're wealthy on blood money."

"Among other things, including shares in several wineries in Tricemore, at least twenty merchant companies, and several rock quarries. They've been trying to marry into a better title for years. Tesly uniting with Fathoms Deep would be the match of the century."

"So where is he?"

"To your right, back two tables, olive skin, blue hair. He married when he was remarkably young, gave birth to twins shortly before divorcing his husband only three years later. Lord Kamir retained exclusive rights to the children. That's one of the reasons they think Lesto will eventually approach him."

"Children?" Shemal asked, stomach giving a lurch when Bani nodded. Suddenly that brief conversation they'd had while escaping Lesto's kidnappers didn't seem so strange or random. Of course Lesto would want—need—children, and marrying someone who already had them was a good idea. Shemal had always taken it for granted that if he settled down and wanted children, he could just adopt them from someone else in his family. It was a fairly common practice given the polyamorous traditions of the island, the way the whole community raised children instead of the isolated way preferred by Mainlanders. Not that he thought Lesto would ever go so far as to marry him... but if he did... would adopting Islander children be acceptable?

His heart started pounding fit to burst, and Shemal

hastily shoved all his wild thoughts aside before he succumbed to the urge to run back to his cottage and goats, to the boring, ordinary life he knew how to handle.

"He's definitely a better choice than the fluffy boy," Shemal said.

Bani snickered. "You really do sound like Lesto. Lord Kamir's family has been pining after the Fathoms Deep match for years; rumor has it that's what they wanted all along, but Lord Kamir ruined it when he insisted on marrying for love."

"Worse reasons to marry. Pity it didn't work out for him," Shemal said. He eyed Kamir, who was positively breathtaking, as much as Shemal hated to admit it. His hair was dyed a dark, rich blue, which must have cost a fortune, and fell to his shoulders in soft waves. He smiled shyly at Shemal and gave a slight nod before turning his attention back to the book set out in front of him.

Huh. Kamir acted more like an ally than a rival. Shemal snorted. Rival. Yes. That was what he was, a rival for Lesto's hand in the High Court. Mother Ocean, the fancy life was already going to his head.

Shemal turned back to Tecilia, who dropped his gaze when he saw Shemal looking, curling his fingers tightly around the spoon in his hand.

It was like looking over a lineup of guppy sailors and trying to pick out the ones that were going to harass him because they hated Islanders—an attitude that either vanished quickly as they realized how stupid they were, or got them killed in a hurry because sailors who couldn't cooperate didn't last long.

He focused on his lunch as Bani kept rambling about other lords and ladies, gossip, parties, festivals, more information to be added to the chaos spinning through his head. It was almost a relief when they finished because she switched back to explaining the palace itself as they walked through it, and that was somewhat easier to deal with than all the people.

They'd just finished looking at something she'd called the Blue Night Garden when a familiar voice caught Shemal as fiercely as a riptide. "—one good reason I shouldn't crack your heads like a walnut! When I put you in charge of patrols, I meant for you to take charge and supervise my soldiers, act like the fucking officers I am trusting you to be! Not dally at a pub talking to a nice pair of tits. By the time I'm done with the lot of you, you're never going to want—"

Lesto broke off as he realized the soldiers he was tearing apart were looking past him and whipped around—and all the tension drained from his shoulders. The anger on his face turned into a smile. "Shemal. You look rested." Without sparing the soldiers so much as a glance, acting for all the world like they were no longer there, Lesto strode across the yard to join Shemal and Bani. "I hope your day is going well. Thank you again, Bani, for showing him around."

Bani bowed. "It's been a pleasure, Commander. So far we've had an excellent day, I think."

"Good," he said gruffly then turned back to Shemal. "I assume you've had lunch?"

Shemal nodded. Lesto looked eminently kissable, but he was pretty sure he'd get punched for doing that in front of men Lesto was two steps from killing. "Should I let you finish eviscerating your soldiers?"

Lesto made a face, but instead of looking back at the soldiers, he turned and motioned to a man Shemal hadn't noticed before. "Jader."

Jader crossed the yard to join them. He was even thinner than Lesto and had skin the color of snow. Shemal would have thought he was sick except it had too much healthy luster to it, and he looked fit in every other way. He was slightly taller than Lesto, with pale brown eyes and hair as black as his skin was white, short and plastered to his skull. He wore the uniform of the imperial army, even the leather armor he wouldn't need working in the palace all day. Strangely, he had two swords, one at each hip. Like Lesto, he had a presence about, even when doing nothing, that practically shouted he was in charge and would brook no argument.

Gripping the man's shoulder tightly, Lesto said, "This is Deputy High Commander Jader Star, my second in command and the poor bastard soon to be taking my place."

Surprise filled Jader's face. "Soon to be? You're actually going to retire, old dog?"

"Watch it, pup," Lesto said, but with a smile. He shook Jader's shoulder then let go. "This is Shemal shey Variago, my lover."

Jader grinned, flicked his nose with the middle knuckle of one finger. "From what I hear, everyone is going with Lord Shemal." He extended one hand, palm up.

Startled, Shemal accepted it, wrapping his fingers lightly around Jader's wrist.

"Well met," Jader said in perfect Islander. He grinned at Shemal's surprise. *"I know, I'm way too pasty to be allowed on a beach. I washed up on one as a child, actually, when the ship I was on wrecked. They tried to make me the right color, but it never worked. I just come out looking like a cooked lobster. My mother*

still despairs."

"You're the beached fish from the Belarigo family. I've heard of you but never that you climbed this high in the imperial army. Then again, I don't go home much."

"Neither do I. My mother is pleased with me, but my father and brothers less so. That's one of the reasons I go by Star instead of Belarigo." Jader shrugged and withdrew his hand. *"I think Lesto is collecting Islanders."*

"I don't know what you just said, but you can fuck off," Lesto retorted. He jerked a thumb over his shoulder. "Go do something that will make them cry for the next twelve hours and leave them unable to move for the next twelve days. I want them to remember their suffering for a long time."

Jader smirked. "I've been well-trained in punishing stupid, lazy soldiers, Commander. I have it under control."

"You'd better."

Rolling his eyes, Jader replied, "Go play with your pirate. Or go break the news of your retirement to His Majesty. I wish I could be there to see his face, but I'm afraid he might kill me to delay the matter." He saluted Lesto, bowed to Shemal and Bani, then turned and started snarling at the soldiers who, from the way they flinched, had clearly started to think they might get off lightly since Lesto was distracted.

Lesto walked with Shemal and Bani out of the room. "You're free to go, Bani. We'll find you later if we need you again. Thank you for attending him."

"My pleasure, Commander." She bowed and left, waving at Shemal in farewell.

Shemal stared at him. "Um—"

He was spared figuring out how to ask if he was allowed to kiss Lesto by the firm press of Lesto's mouth, a familiar, possessive hand curling into his hair. Shemal fanned his hands across Lesto's back, keeping him in place but not grabbing and rubbing the way he'd like. He was fairly certain if they did that where people could see them, Lesto really would kill him.

Eventually drawing back, he smiled and said, "I wasn't sure I was allowed to do that."

"Not when I'm yelling at halfwits, but otherwise, always," Lesto replied then smiled, a familiar glint in his eye. "Come on, there's something I want to show you."

Lust curled slow and lazy through Shemal, a satisfying heat he was content to let burn and build as he walked alongside Lesto through the halls of the palace.

"I hope you've had a good day so far."

"Hard to have a bad day when it's really only involved sleeping, eating, and walking." Shemal smiled slowly. "Would have been better if I'd gotten to do what I wanted when I woke up, but I guess that's what I get for waking up late."

Lesto laughed and squeezed his arm. "That would have been vastly preferable to being dragged out of bed because of those halfwits I was yelling at. I'd only just let them out of the stocks when you showed up. They probably think they're getting off lightly because Jader is handling their punishment now."

"They think they'll get off lightly because they're being disciplined by a white-skinned Islander who climbed all the way to Deputy High Commander?" Shemal let out a sharp bark of laughter. "I'd rather piss off Penance Gate again."

Lesto gave a wolfish smile. "Just so."

"The High King didn't have issue with an Islander becoming so powerful?"

"Why would Sarrica care? He's no bigger a fan of conscription and the general hatred for Farlanders than I am. We've been working to fix it for years. That aside, Sarrica cares only that things run smoothly so they're not one more problem for him to deal with. He has no complaints with Jader, though that might change once they have to start working more closely together." He smirked. "I can't wait to enjoy watching that from afar."

"Why are you retiring?" Shemal asked.

Lesto sighed. "Because I'm tired, and envious that everyone around me has gotten to step back and settle down. Even Sarrica is not as busy as he used to be, or at least, he's more cheerful about being that busy. I barely see my own estates, and now there is a lover for whom I would like to make time. Though I'd already decided to retire before you and I crossed paths again."

"So you don't have to because of me?"

Lesto stopped, stared at him. "No, though if that was necessary, I would have done it. I've been High Commander a long time, and a soldier nearly all my life. I wouldn't mind being something else with what remains of my life. Now come on, I think you'll like what I want you to see."

Though Shemal had no idea where they were, he had a pretty good idea where they were going. "Would it happen to be a certain room where I once behaved indecently with the High Commander?"

Lesto threw a grin over his shoulder but didn't say anything or stop walking.

A few minutes later he unlocked a door Shemal still saw in his dreams. He still heard that sound too, the soft but thunderous click of the door closing. The snick of a turning key was new. Lesto grabbed the front of his shirt and yanked him close. Shemal would never get tired of the way they were the same height, the way he could meet that mouth directly, brace his hands on the door and focus on devouring, not the strain in his neck from having to lean down or the burn of his muscles from hefting someone up. He drew back briefly to say, "I feel we're ignoring an important lesson about fucking in empty rooms where anyone could find us."

"You might not have learned anything, but I locked the door and came prepared."

Shemal laughed and went back to kissing him, feeding and sucking at Lesto's mouth until they were both breathing heavily. Finally drawing back, he pulled Lesto away from the door and dragged him into the center of the room. Last time, Lesto had pushed him onto the small sofa against one wall, climbed atop him, and rutted like they were youths still learning how their cocks worked. He'd made Shemal feel like he was that young again.

Then Lesto had dragged him to the floor and growled for Shemal to fuck him. Shemal had nearly lost it right then and there. If he'd thought about it, which back then he definitely hadn't, he would have expected an order to spread. That was how powerful types usually behaved with someone like him. Not Lesto, though; he was one breathtaking, mind-melting surprise after another.

"I'm surprised you want to drag me here when you have a bed the size of a house we could be using,"

Shemal said, nibbling at his jaw as he slid one hand down to cup Lesto through his breeches. "I'm also surprised you've forgotten what a pain in the ass it is getting you out of that belt and all those layers."

"I'm fairly confident it's worth the aggravation," Lesto retorted—then grabbed him and did some twisty-throw move that put Shemal on his back with all the breath knocked out of him.

Any chance of getting that breath back was ruined as Lesto straddled him. He spanned his hands over Lesto's thighs—and felt the bulk of bandages. "You shouldn't—"

"I swear to the Pantheon if you say a single word about my injuries, I will leave you suffering for a long time," Lesto cut in then set to work removing his clothes. "I was looking forward to seeing you in that jacket I picked out, but I admit I like what you went with even better."

Shemal snorted, though the compliment warmed him far more than even the lust. "You just appreciate the easy access to your mark on my skin, you possessive ass. Get *your* clothes off—I remember never being able to sort out all those buckles and straps. I could hear you coming from the far side of the pavilion, despite all the other noise."

Lesto smirked as he pulled away and stood. "I like to watch everyone flee or cower." He made quick and easy work of removing his sword belt, tunic, leather armor, and the quilted tunic beneath that.

"Yet you expect anyone to believe that you're going to retire and give up that thrill."

Tossing aside the last of his layers, Lesto resumed straddling Shemal's lap, rubbing and grinding against him. "I'll settle for the new thrill of being able to stay in bed as long as I want and not being dragged from it at all hours."

Shemal laughed, but it came out ragged as Lesto shifted enough to work on removing the breeches Shemal hadn't gotten to because he'd been too busy admiring Lesto.

His clothes were barely stripped away when Lesto was back, mouth dropping over Shemal's cock like a crashing wave. Shemal groaned, head falling sharply to thud against the floor as his hips worked to thrust his cock even deeper into that hot, far-too-talented mouth. *"Mother Ocean, who made you a* noble instead of a whore?"

Lesto pulled off his cock, dragged his tongue across Shemal's abdomen. "I'm not nice enough to have been a whore, if that's what you were asking." He straddled Shemal once more, rising up on his knees and getting hold of Shemal's cock.

Shemal started to ask if he was crazy when he slid into tight, slick heat. He groaned, almost came right then, picturing Lesto walking around slick and ready, just waiting for Shemal to show up. "You're the best kind of evil."

Laughing raggedly, Lesto sank all the way down on his cock, leaving them both gasping and shivering. After a moment, with Shemal's hands curled firmly around his hips, Lesto began to move, rising up and sinking slowly back down, increasing the pace steadily, never succumbing to impatience or haste.

Eventually Shemal could take no more of the exquisite torture and gave a last few sharp thrusts up into Lesto's body before coming with a cry he barely bit back. Lesto followed him shortly after, jerking at his cock and spilling over his hand and Shemal's skin.

When Shemal could breathe properly again and Lesto had slid off to sit beside him, he propped himself on his elbows and said, "I am fairly certain we said we wouldn't be doing this again. Something about being far too old for nonsense and hard floors."

Lesto shrugged, mouth quirking at one end. "I certainly have no plans to make this a habit, but it seemed appropriate."

Shemal couldn't deny that. "I don't suppose you brought something to clean up with."

Smiling, Lesto rose and went to the small table by the door, opened one of the drawers, and tossed Shemal some cloths.

"You really did plot this," Shemal said with a laugh as he stood and cleaned up. He closed the space between them, pushed Lesto up against the door, and took his fill of that warm, pliant mouth before drawing away to clean Lesto up. "What would the imperial army say if they knew their commander was spending his time planning assignations instead of working?"

"They'd hope that meant they could get away with something," Lesto replied and kissed him again before slipping away to get dressed. When they were both ready, and almost looked like they hadn't just been fucking, Lesto unlocked the door and led him down yet another hall. "There's something else I want to show you."

Shemal nodded, more interested in the way they walked close enough together that their hands kept brushing, reminding him of the time in the garrison where Lesto had walked off *holding* his hand. "Bani pointed out a couple of your friends today."

"Friends?" Lesto's brow drew down. "You've met all my friends, save those not on the premises."

"Maybe I should say marriage prospects."

"Oh, *them.*" Lesto shook his head. "Did Lord Tecilia spend all his time glaring at you and clutching his spoon like he wished it was a knife?"

Shemal chuckled. "Yes, actually. What is he, fifteen?"

Lesto smirked. "Twenty or so, I think, though his attitude is certainly closer to fifteen. What did you think of Lord Kamir?"

"He seemed decent and deserves better than to be a tool, though I know that's how you people do it."

Shrugging, Lesto replied, "Yes, but most people try to make sure couples will be happy together. Lord Kamir is a good man, but he and I decided a long time ago we were not compatible. I am relatively certain he is pining after a different commander, anyway."

"Commander Jader?" Shemal laughed when Lesto nodded. "I'm starting to see why gossip is such a thing. It could get addictive, tracking all the little pieces and goings on."

Lesto shook his head, smiling faintly. "I have a feeling you will get on well with Allen and Tara. Those two thrive on playing the game that is High Court, and Allen is certainly the master of the game. People train for years just to be able to live here for a few months, and those that remain here full time are not to be trifled with. I am not looking forward to dealing with it more once I retire, but so it goes. Here we are."

Shemal's questions fell away as they walked through a large open archway into the biggest room he'd ever seen. Most of the enormous space had been taken over by a gigantic bathing pool. There were plants and flowers all around the perimeter, and the area immediately around the pool was paved with colorful stones. The ceiling was glass, clear and beautiful, save for the very center, which was made of yellow glass in a sunburst design. "What is this?"

"It used to be a bathing pool, back when the public baths were located in this wing," Lesto replied. "It fell into disuse until Jader, actually, suggested making it what he called a swimming pool. It's quiet now, but usually it is filled with Farlanders, sailors, other soldiers and visitors who grew up around water. There's a festival or something Farlanders celebrate at the end of summer. They always gather here for it." Lesto snorted. "And sleep here because they're too drunk to return to their own rooms."

"The Festival of Mother Ocean," Shemal replied. "It's a celebration of women. One of our most important holidays." He smiled at Lesto. "Bad luck not to receive a kiss from a woman on the Ocean's day." He looked back at the pool, took a few steps closer. The air was a bit warmer than the rest of the palace had been. In the pool itself, the water was clear as glass, and so still that only the way the sun reflected made it visible at all. The walls and bottom of the pool were made of colorful tiles, formed into mosaics of fish, ships, suns, moons, and other marks of the ocean and sailing.

In the middle of the mosaic were his islands. Their actual name was a source of debate, alternately called the Broken Ends and the Lost Lands in various written and oral accounts. That was back when they'd still been part of the country of Pemfrost. Then Pemfrost had broken into three, and the Broken Ends became their own entity, largely forgotten by the war-busy Mainland. Eventually, Gearth had broken in half, creating the Outlands, and they'd remembered the far, forgotten islands and started paying attention to them again.

Which had made exactly nobody happy, and now they were the Farlands.

"You can go for a swim if you like," Lesto said. "Unless it's not of interest after all?"

Shemal turned as Lesto drew up beside him. "Oh, it's of interest. Once I get in that water, you'll have a hard time getting me back out. I'd rather see more of the palace for now, though. Find something useful to do with myself." Or maybe he'd find a way to improve his reading and writing abilities before everyone found out he was atrocious at both. Learning to speak Harken had been difficult enough, especially since he'd pushed himself to master formal Harken. There hadn't been time for more than the most basic lessons in reading and writing, something only people with plenty of time and money could afford.

"There's no rush," Lesto replied. "Acclimating to palace life is hard enough. I'm sure you'll fall into something eventually. If nothing else, I can put you in charge of punching important people who need to have a lesson or six driven into them."

"I'm fairly certain I've escaped a death sentence twice now for punching important people, and my luck won't hold forever."

Laughing, Lesto turned and motioned for Shemal to follow him, threading back toward the main portions of the palace as he suggested things for Shemal to see and do, until someone eventually appeared to drag Lesto away.

CHAPTER SEVEN

Lesto didn't bother to look up when somebody knocked on his door. "I'm pretty damned certain I said I wasn't to be disturbed by anyone, up to and including Sarrica."

"Well, too damned bad," Sarrica drawled. "I'm High King, my orders overrule yours."

Lesto groaned. "Get the fuck out of my office. I'm trying to get work done. My estates do actually need me to pay attention to them upon occasion."

Sarrica snorted. "No, they're much happier when they don't have your over-controlling tendencies leaning over their shoulder snarling at them."

Lesto threw down the papers he'd been holding. "What do you want?"

Stepping into the office, Sarrica closed the door, then leaned against it. "When are you actually going to *tell* me what I've been hearing for the past four days?"

"You're bothering me while I'm trying to get work done because you're sulking I haven't explicitly said *I'm retiring?* It's not like I needed to tell *you*." Nobody knew Lesto better than Sarrica, which meant he'd probably known Lesto was ready to quit long before Lesto.

Sarrica sighed. "The courtesy would have been nice."

"Ha," Lesto retorted. "This from the man who did nothing but whine about how handsome I looked when I got my eye stabbed out of my face."

"Stop exaggerating. It was a slice, not a stab." Sarrica pushed away from the door and dropped into the chair next to it. "So are you going to return to Fathoms Deep?"

Lesto leaned back in his own chair. "For a little while, so Jader can take over without everyone trying to run to me every time he does something a little different. But never fear, for all I want to spend time at Fathoms Deep, I wouldn't know what to do with myself without the barely contained chaos of this place. And Allen would kill me if I wasn't around to occasionally distract you so he can work."

Sarrica gestured crudely. He stretched out his legs and draped his arms over the rests. "Should I be figuring out a suitable wedding gift?"

"We've only been lovers a matter of weeks, and Shemal is still acclimating to life here, so would people stop trying to rush us into vows?" Lesto rubbed at his temples. "On second thought, I think I will remove permanently to Fathoms Deep, and you can all go jump in the ocean for all I care."

"I know you think I'm stupid," Sarrica said idly, "but I know the look of an Arseni when their mind is made up. Give me *some* credit, Lesto."

Lesto wanted to throw something at him. "The point remains that barely any time has passed. A mind made up doesn't mean action should be taken. If you or anyone else even thinks about harassing Shemal, I will drag you—"

"I'm not going to do anything to your precious pirate," Sarrica cut in, lifting his hands and rolling his eyes. "I will do my level best to piss you off, but when don't I do that?" He smiled.

Lesto smiled briefly back. "I still don't see why you're bothering me about this now. It could have waited until I wasn't busy."

"I had another reason. The last of the Treya Mencee delegates scattered around the empire arrived today. I put them all in separate rooms, appointed guards to watch them, and came to harass you until I decided they'd been left to suffer long enough. Also to see if you wanted to interview them with me, or if you were too busy playing at Lord Lesto today."

"Those bastards tried to have me and Shemal killed. Of course I want to interview them," Lesto replied. "Why are you asking such a stupid question?"

Sarrica shrugged. "Thought you might be pulling away from such nonsense. Try to remember I need them alive for now."

"For now," Lesto muttered and began sorting the scattered stacks of papers on his desk, piling things at the edge for his secretaries to take away, the other stacks for him to resume working on whenever he was allowed near his desk again. Standing, he lifted his sword belt from where he'd hung it over the back of his chair. "Have they been left to stew long enough?"

"By the time we get to the meeting room they will have," Sarrica said. "Allen is already feeling out new sugar contracts since our arrangements with Treya Mencee are definitely not going to be intact by the end of this mess. He wanted to attend this meeting, but he's so pre-occupied with shifting the sugar contracts, and a few others, that he couldn't come. There's so much money involved I even wince thinking about it."

Lesto shrugged. "Trey Mencee shouldn't have slaughtered an entire ship and then tried to kidnap me. There are two other countries eager to sell us sugar. It's Treya Mencee that stands to lose from this, not us."

"Let's go see just how much they're willing to lose, then," Sarrica said and pulled open the office door.

Lesto's secretaries ducked back to their work, like they hadn't been trying to listen to what was going on in Lesto's office. Though his people were loyal, gossip was the currency of the imperial palace, and gossip about Sarrica and Lesto could practically fetch a king's ransom.

They strode through the halls, people hastening to get out of their way. "Why don't you have bodyguards with you?" Lesto asked. "How many times do we have to discuss this?"

Sarrica rolled his eyes. "I can't wait for you to retire because then you'll no longer be able to nag incessantly about my bodyguards."

"I can still remind you as any good friend would," Lesto replied, his smile all teeth as Sarrica groaned.

"I was just going down two small hallways," Sarrica groused. "I hardly needed bodyguards for that. Now I'm with you, so the point is moot. You know, once you're a civilian, you'll need bodyguards, too, given you're part of the imperial family and can no longer hide behind 'but I'm the High Commander.'"

Lesto scowled. "I do not—"

"Aha!" Sarrica said, giving him a shove. "Fucking hypocrite. See how annoying it is?"

Lesto shoved him right back. "Stuff it."

Sarrica laughed as he barely avoided slamming into a wall. The few remaining people in the hall made quick exits, leaving only Fathoms Deep, who were long used to the antics of their High King and High

Commander. "Get as mad as you want, but if you expect me to drag around bodyguards, you're going to have to do the same."

"Shut up," Lesto muttered. "So we've gathered Treya Mencee. Where in the Realms is Lord Bestowen?"

"He should be here in another day or so, I think. He's been damnably hard to pin down. The bastard wasn't at home, even though by all accounts, he should have been. In a positively shocking twist of coincidence, he was in Gearth on unexpected business. From what I've read even the most apathetic halfwit could tell his reasons were contrived. Once we've beaten information out of Treya Mencee, we'll figure out what he was really doing and what he has to do with the whole mess. Speaking of things I still don't know but would really like to: how do you and your pirate come to know one another so well you want to marry the man mere weeks after reuniting?"

"I have yet to say anything about marriage; stop listening to palace gossip." Lesto cast him a warning look, for all the good it would do.

"I *don't* listen to palace gossip, and you damn well know it," Sarrica replied. "I told you, I'm not stupid. I know how you Arsenis look when your minds are made up, and you've been wearing that look from the moment I saw the two of you together at the garrison. Rene was gone on Tara days after they were together, and Nyle fought it, but he admitted later his mind had been made up from the start. You've always been three times more decisive than those two. So quit trying to play me for a halfwit and tell me the details about how you met because there was obviously a great deal more to the matter than him punching you."

"I intend to go to my pyre with the rest of the story, so you may as well quit asking."

Sarrica cast him a look, and Lesto could almost see his mind spinning, spinning. There were plenty of people who took Sarrica to be a fool because he was a soldier who had no patience for the finer points of court, because he had a short temper and a knack for saying the wrong thing at the worst time. Those people always learned too late how wrong they were; Sarrica was rude, impatient, and temperamental, but he wasn't stupid.

Lesto sighed in resignation as he saw the moment Sarrica figured it out.

"You fucked him, didn't you? He punched you, and you snuck off to fuck him." Sarrica looked like someone had just handed him the greatest treasure in the world. "You delinquent bastard, I didn't know you had it in you." His eyes took on a gleam, mouth curving into a smirk. "Although I bet you did, in fact, have it—"

Lest shoved him into the wall. "How about you shut your damned mouth before I kill you. I really don't need more rumors going about the palace, so keep your voice down. I don't know why I put up with you."

"Please, what the court doesn't know they are just as happy to make up, and usually that's worse. If you keep shoving me around, the rumors of us fucking are going to resurface."

"Do they ever vanish?" Lesto groused.

Sarrica made a face, and Lesto could follow his thoughts easily enough: all the trouble Sarrica and Allen had suffered at the beginning of their relationship would have been infinitely worse if Allen had arrived when the rumors of Sarrica and Lesto sleeping together had been on the rise instead of the ebb. As it was, Allen just found them amusing.

"We're not done with this conversation," Sarrica said.

"Oh, yes we are." Lesto paused as they reached the doors of the room where they were meeting the Treya Mencee delegation—both those assigned to Harkenesten, and those gathered from around the empire, where they'd been assigned to various palaces. Looking at the guards, he said, "Bring in the delegates, but one at a time. I don't want them to see each other until they're in this room. Save Ambassador Lace for last. I want him ready to piss himself."

"Yes, Commander," the guard said and, with a bow, departed.

Sarrica strode into the room and down the length of it to the chair at the head of the table. Sitting with all the idleness only a High King could possess in such a situation, he said, "I'm surprised Shemal wasn't in your office. I would have let him sit in on the meeting if he wanted. Should we have him summoned?"

"Don't bother. Lord Tara returned to Harkenesten last night and they met this morning," Lesto replied wryly. "When I left they already seemed to be fast friends."

"Uh-oh." Sarrica grinned.

Lesto nodded. "I expect we'll start hearing complaints before the day ends. The High Court is less than amused than Allen now counts his closest friends the court eccentric and a former pirate."

"You'll be lucky if those two don't go off pirating together," Sarrica replied. "I've no doubt Allen would be happy to fund the venture as long as they promised to send him gifts."

"I'm hoping they'll settle for wreaking havoc in court." Lesto gave him a look. "You'd better hope they keep it to a minimum or you'll be inundated in complaints about what your consort and his dubious friends are doing."

"They'll stop whining at me after I slap fines on them." Sarrica's grin widened as he enjoyed whatever images were filling his head. "My golden tongue, an eccentric, and a pirate. I wish I had time to simply sit and watch them turn the High Court upside down."

Lesto pinched his eyes closed. "I am definitely going to Fathoms Deep and never returning."

Sarrica laughed hard enough his body shook with it, startling the servant who'd just entered, pushing a cart laden with food and drink. When she'd set everything on the table and gone, he said, "You never should have let Tara and Shemal meet, but I'm not sorry they did."

The door opened again, bringing the conversation to a halt, and both men banished their levity and settled into their roles and the severity of the situation. They sat in stony silence as, one-by-one, the guards brought in all fifteen delegates. Counting their families and staff, the total number was significantly higher, but the problem more than likely lay in one of the fifteen people in that room.

As they all settled into place, pouring wine or tea, the door opened one last time, and a silver tongue came bustling in, murmuring apologies as she bowed and sat opposite Lesto.

"Let's begin, shall we?" Sarrica said. "You'll forgive me for not being in the mood for pleasantries. You are here because I want to know who is responsible for the slaughter of three hundred and twenty crewmen, fifty mercenaries, and thirty-three passengers, as well as the kidnapping and attempted murder of my High Commander."

Lord Lace, the Treya Mencee ambassador—and therefore the man responsible for the actions of every other person at the table—leaned forward in his seat, mouth pinched and eyes tight as he said, "You have no evidence that Treya Mencee had anything to do those matters. All my people are accounted for; not a one of them could have arranged such things anyway."

"Don't underestimate the resourcefulness of the desperate," Lesto said. "As to evidence, how about we let you be the judge? Everyone on board was murdered in the exact same way, save those who were capable of fighting back: throats slit with a serrated blade, and half of them also had their right hands cut off."

Lace's already pale skin went sickly, and everyone else at the table looked equally unhappy and ill at ease.

"I have it on good authority," Lesto continued, "that such a grisly practice is a long-standing tradition of the Hands of Death, who answer exclusively to the royal family of Treya Mencee. Am I wrong?"

Lace's lips were pressed so tightly together they'd gone white.

Sarrica barked, "Is he wrong?"

"No, Your Majesty, High Commander. That sounds exactly like the Hands of Death. But if Treya Mencee took issue with Harken, they would have tried diplomatic means first. We are well aware of what a positive relationship with Harken brings us and have no wish to jeopardize it. If they were sending out the Hands of Death, whom they would never send to foreign soil, they would have warned me, and I vow they have not."

"What of the rest of those gathered here? Would they have knowledge of such a thing, knowledge they would not share with you?"

"Not if they wished to remain alive," Lace replied flatly, causing several people to flinch and look closer to panicking than ever.

But none of them acted *guilty.* They acted like people who were afraid they would be blamed no matter what the truth of the matter might be. Lesto swept his gaze back and forth, watching them closely as Sarrica started laying into them again, detailing all that had happened to Lesto from the kidnapping onward.

When Sarrica came to the tavern where Lesto and Shemal had been attacked, the young man at the far end, three seats from Lace, looked angry and miserable for the barest moment. It wasn't much of a tell, but it was certainly enough to poke at.

Lesto smacked his hand on the table lightly, halting the conversation. Sarrica leaned back and waited for him to proceed. Gesturing at the young man in question, Lesto looked at Lace and asked, "Who is he? What does he do?"

"He is my assistant," Lace said. "Peter Tarn. He is the youngest son of a good friend of mine. I'm training him as a favor. He's a boy, harmless."

That was no boy. That was a young man, at least twenty years of age, plenty old enough to get in way over his head. "Who is this good friend?"

"Lady Vesper, Marchioness of Whitley. She's..." Lace stopped speaking, some sort of awful realization falling over his face. His gaze snapped back to Peter, and he started speaking in rapid Treyan.

Lesto and Sarrica looked at the silver tongue, who started speaking while watching the conversation on the far side of the table. "He wants to know what Peter's brother has done this time, what mess has he dragged Peter into." She frowned. "Peter says that the Star of Menceera is missing, that the Hands of Death were sent to take it back and kill everyone on the ship as a warning to the thief, but the Star wasn't on board. Peter tried to stop them, but it was too late by the time his messages reached Treya Mencee. His brother also ordered their own men to—"

She stopped as Lace broke off, rose, and went around the table to yank Peter from his seat and started hitting the boy back and forth across the face. Lesto surged from his seat and closed the distance quickly. He tore them apart, threw Lace on the floor, and pushed Peter back in his chair. Drawing his sword, he planted a boot on Lace's chest and said, "I can tell you from experience that beating information out of people is a last resort and should be done with more care than you are showing. Are you going to behave, or do I need to summon guards?"

"You don't understand," Lace said. "His brother sent out Blood of the Fallen. That is their family's private guard, and while not as violent and murderous as the Hands of Death, they are ruthless to a fault."

Lesto's eye narrowed, the hot anger running through his blood steadily heating to rage. "Do they wear red leather armor trimmed in gold?"

"Yes," Lace said. "They shouldn't even be here. The Hands of Death, Blood of the Fallen—they deal with *internal* matters. They are not allowed to operate outside the country. It's simply too dangerous. Like letting a wild dog off its chain. They are infinitely valuable back home. Treya Mencee is a violent place and needs must, but we don't use them abroad. If they've been ordered to bring in Bestowen and retrieve the Star of Menceera, they will keep going until they accomplish that mission."

Lesto looked to Peter. "Call off your dogs."

"I can't," Peter said. "My brother is the only one who can command them, the only one they'll listen to. I can advise, but I don't have the authority to call them off. If I tried, they would simply ignore me. I didn't want them to come along, but my brother ordered it, so they snuck aboard as part of the regular army sent to serve as our bodyguards."

"No one noticed all these men were missing?" Lesto snarled at Lace. "Ten men attacked us in that fucking tavern. You were permitted an escort of fifty men. You didn't notice ten of them weren't where they should be?"

Lace's mouth tightened. "No, I've been pre-occupied and left Peter to tend such matters for me. I mistakenly trusted he would tell me if something was wrong."

Lesto snarled, sheathed his sword, bent, and yanked Lace to his feet, threw him toward his chair. "Tell me right now how to stop Blood of the Fallen."

"Get back the Star of Menceera," Peter said. "Or kill them. You've killed ten, but there are fifteen more."

Striding to the door, Lesto grabbed the handle—and was nearly whacked in the face as the door flew open. He stumbled back, slamming into the wall, and snarled, "What do you think you're doing?"

"Commander!" The guard snapped to attention,

wide-eyed with dismay. "You must come at once. Lord Shemal got into an altercation with Lord Tecilia and wound up breaking Lord Tecilia's arm. His family is furious, and Lord Shemal has run off. Lord Tara was there and went after him, but we don't know where they've gone."

"Damn it!" Lesto bellowed. He gestured sharply at the Treya Mencee delegates. "Arrest all of them. I don't care where you shove them, but they're not to be held together. Someone locate Lord Bestowen and have him here by morning, or heads will start rolling."

More guards came in at a signal from the first, and Lesto jabbed fingers at two of them. "You are not to leave His Majesty's side until I bid you do otherwise, I don't care what he says. If you defy me, I will put you in stocks for the rest of the year. Am I understood?"

"Yes, Commander!"

"Where is Lord Tecilia right now?"

"The sunset room."

Lesto stormed off, motioning to two more guards in the hallway who fell into step behind him without hesitation. He cut down servant stairs then all but ran the length of a dark, narrow hallway to the compass hall, then started up yet another hallway that would take him to the public areas where the sunset room was located.

He saw a group of nobles fluttering around the hall as he turned the corner. When they saw him, they all blanched and fled. Lesto stepped into the sunset room and looked around at all the broken furniture, the blood on the carpet. His stomach churned, a dull ache spreading through his chest, tangling with the anger that burned ever hotter.

"Commander!" Tecilia's father, Lord Ketherow,

rose from the armchair he was sitting in, angry and arrogant, but with a gleam of triumph Lesto knew all too well—the triumph of a schemer who'd found a weakness to exploit that would get him everything he wanted. "I demand recompense for this terrible—"

"So terrible that instead of immediately taking your son to the healer, you leave him sitting here in pain so you can extract what, money? A promise of marriage?" Lesto moved forward like a predator on the hunt, grabbed Ketherow around the throat, and slammed him into the wall. "You have exactly ten seconds to tell me what really happened here, or I will throw the whole lot of you in a cell where you can rot until I feel like remembering you exist. Not only have you attacked my lover, a man called friend by the High Throne, you have taken me away from a matter that will result in the deaths of hundreds of people, unless I stop it. If those people die, you will be convicted of willfully endangering the empire." He squeezed tighter then threw Ketherow to the floor. "Start talking."

His demeanor decidedly less arrogant and affronted, Ketherow said, "I wasn't here to witness what happened. Guards summoned me after the fact. Tecilia said they were arguing—"

"I told him all the ways he was ruining your life by pretending to be something he wasn't, the way somebody else already should have!" Tecilia snarled. "He's a pirate, Farlander trash, pretending to be a lord, like he's someone you'd actually keep for long when any halfwit can see he's just some plaything. Everyone says you're going to marry him, and that sort of nonsense can't be allowed to—" He stopped as Lesto prowled toward him.

"You hit him right where it would hurt most, just

like the petty, vindictive child you are," Lesto said. "Even if any of that was true, which it's not, it wasn't your place to say such things, and you damn well know it. He *isn't* ruining my life; you're just a jealous brat. I *am* going to marry him, so if I were you, I'd start practicing how you're going to apologize to him if you and your family ever want to be allowed back in the High Court. What provoked the fight? Shemal wouldn't have turned violet over that."

Tecilia's mouth pinched, eyes dropping to the floor. "Lord Tara attempted to interfere in the conversation, and I told him exactly what everyone thinks of *him*."

"My, my, you are quite the chatty little fool, aren't you? Then what? Shemal doesn't break arms over insults, especially insults spouted off by children."

"He *laughed* at me," Tecilia said petulantly. "I struck him, as was my right, but then Lord Berry jumped him from behind and Rister—"

"Three of you jumped him because he laughed at you?" Lesto said. "No wonder he broke your fucking arm. You're lucky you didn't suffer worse, going up against a man who has survived tangling with Penance Gate and worse. What sort of rampant stupidity convinces three soft nobles to get into a fight with a former pirate—a former pirate who has punched both the High Commander and the High King. Did you really think you were going to best him?" He turned to Ketherow, who looked about half a step away from passing out. "Your family is banned from Harkenesten for six months. I highly suggest that when you return, you leave your son behind—unless he somehow manages to grow up. You will not warn the other parties involved, and you should probably expect His

Majesty to add his own punishments to the pile. You should be ash—"

He broke off at the sound of boots pounding down the hallway and turned just as a guard appeared in the doorway, heaving for breath, skin flushed red and dripping sweat. "Commander, come at once to His Majesty's office."

Lesto swore. "Find more guards, escort Lord Tecilia to the healers, then escort him and Lord Ketherow to their rooms and supervise their packing. They're to be out of the palace by nightfall. The same goes for Ziirin and Bremer. If they give you trouble, tell Jader I want them made to suffer. Am I understood?"

"Yes, Commander!"

"Good. See to it Sarrica's secretaries draft the banishment papers. Six months, on my command, and whatever Sarrica chooses to add on. If I missed anything, Sarrica or Allen can handle it."

"Yes, Commander."

Lesto swept out of the room and all but ran back through the palace to Sarrica's offices.

Where he was greeted by the sight of a battered, bloody Lord Tara curled up in Rene's arms, Allen sitting on his other side holding one of his hands. Ice-cold fear squeezed his chest. He couldn't *breathe.* "Where—" He broke off, unable to force the question out, terrified what the answer would be.

Sarrica strode across the room and grabbed his shoulders. "He's *alive*, Lesto."

Lesto shuddered, nearly dropping to his knees in relief. He shrugged off Sarrica's hands, but cast him a brief look of gratitude. "Are you all right, Tara?"

"Yes," Tara said. "I don't know how you halfwits do this for a living." He motioned to his bruised, bloody, tear-streaked face. "Food and rest will heal me up fine. It's only because of Shemal that I got away. He got into a fight with Lord Tecilia, who jumped him, and two of his friends right along with him. The guards tried to stop it, but they'd all come prepared, had weights in their fists, and one of them brought out a cane. But it was when Tecilia brought out a dagger—"

"I'm going to kill that—"

"Lesto, calm down. Whatever punishment you've already given them, I'll quadruple it," Sarrica said, holding tightly to Lesto's arm and dragging him back in a way only Sarrica and Rene could do and live to tell the tale.

Tara continued, "That's when Shemal broke his arm, then he panicked and ran. I went after him, all the way to the city. Then everything just went *wrong*. We were grabbed by men in red leather, dragged off." He shook his head. "I thought Shemal had been fighting before, when those brats attacked him, but he was something else entirely fighting off those men in red. He—" His face went a bit gray. "He killed three of them, but some others had me, tried to use me against him. He stopped, they let down their guard, and he killed two more and got me away from them, then fled the other way so they'd go after him since it was definitely him they wanted. I came back here as quickly as I could." He looked down at his hands. "I'm sorry I couldn't do anything."

Lesto barely heard the others comforting him, too busy trying to see past the blinding rage. Even Sarrica's hand on his shoulder didn't help much.

"I've already summoned Lace and Peter," Sarrica said. "They should be here any moment. Do whatever you want short of killing them. Allen can sweet talk our way out of any problems later."

"You make it sound so easy," Allen said with a soft sigh. "It's remarkably hard to do when I want to kill them myself."

Sarrica smiled at him.

Lesto looked away. Damn it, where the fuck—

The door opened and four Fathoms Deep dragged in Peter and Lace, who both looked one step away from killing themselves. "Bring them here," Lesto said, and when they were close enough, he grabbed Peter by the throat and yanked him forward. "I am officially out of patience. Your fucking mercenaries have kidnapped my lover. You will tell me where to find them, or you will wish that Sarrica had given me permission to kill you."

"You can't—do—treaty says—" Peter broke off, looked desperately at Lace, who just stood and watched.

"The treaty says a lot of things that you have seen fit to ignore," Allen said coldly. "I would tread carefully if I were you."

"He did try to stop Blood of the Fallen and the Hands of Death, whatever that is worth," Lace said with a sigh. "The boy deserves to be punished, I'll grant you that, but I don't see what is being accomplished by letting him be thrown about by your out-of-control commander."

Sarrica snorted and leaned against the arm of the sofa Allen and the others sat on, folding his arms across his chest. "If you think Lesto is out of control, you're an even greater a fool than I thought. I keep Lesto as my right hand because he's smart, shrewd, and actually far more patient than me. I made him my High Commander because he is one hundred percent

Arseni, and if that does not frighten you, then your foolishness grows and grows. Tell us what we need to know, or contact your dogs and call them off, or I will send every Treya Mencee head in the empire home in a crate and toss the bodies in the sea."

Lesto squeezed tighter, until Peter wheezed and begged in a thready whisper. "What is the Star of Menceera?"

"A holy relic," Lace said, looking between Lesto and Peter with a look of helpless frustration. "It's cared for and protected by Prince Ravelle. Peter's mother, my friend, has long been Ravelle's paramour. It's rumored he is the actual father of her children, but he's never acknowledged or denied it. Peter said the Star was stolen by Lord Bestowen, or rather, men Bestowen sent to take it. I don't know why yet. But if Ravelle sent out the Hands of Death, then he doesn't want the rest of his family to know it's missing. I'm not exaggerating when I say Her Majesty will kill him and anyone else she suspects of being even passingly involved in the matter. Ravelle is desperate. If Peter's brother sent Blood of the Fallen, then he's party to the mess, or more likely, afraid his family will be blamed no matter what. That relic is important. It's proof the queen and high priestess are fit to rule. If it's discovered missing, the country will devolve into another civil war. The last time the Star went missing, the royal families were wiped out, and the current rulers took the throne largely because they gained possession of the Star."

Sarrica had stood while he talked and strode to the door as he finished. Yanking it open, he barked out, "I want an update on where the fuck Bestowen is, and I want it in five minutes." He slammed the door shut and returned to them. The office had been vacated as some point, so quickly the secretaries hadn't even had a chance to put away all the valuable documents and reports they'd been working on. "Where would the Fallen hole up with a hostage?"

Someone knocked on the door, and Sarrica snarled for them to enter. His head secretary, Myra, stepped into the room, held out a note with one trembling hand. Sarrica started toward him, but with a snarled warning, Lesto threw Peter aside and went to get the note himself. "Are you all right?"

"I'm fine," Myra said. "It was delivered by a boy. He's here, but I doubt he's of use. He's not even ten, if I had to guess. But the note..."

Lesto took it, squeezed Myra's arm in reassurance, and dismissed him. The note was succinct, and all the more chilling for it. *Bring the Star of Menceera or he dies.* The words were followed by a string of coordinates that, if Lesto read them correctly, would put the mercenaries in the ruins north of the palace, right smack between the palace and the Cartha Mountains.

He handed the note off to Sarrica, who read it aloud, save the coordinates.

Allen pursed his lips. "Did it ever once occur to anyone that if we had been contacted, we could have resolved the matter peacefully? That all of this is going to be reported to Her Majesty and all their attempts to keep matters a secret and stay alive were for naught?"

"That's why we tried to keep anyone from figuring out it was Treya Mencee involved," Peter said. "The Fallen went to fetch Bestowen when they thought the other men I'd hired had failed. I did try to keep matters

147

quiet, but the halfwits I hired to bring Bestowen to the Fallen kidnapped the wrong fucking man. Then the Fallen realized it was Commander Lesto they'd actually kidnapped and felt they had no choice but to kill him if there was to be any chance of avoiding a war. Then Commander Lesto killed them and got away..."

"After which there was little point in keeping secrets. They were all going to come out anyway, so now they are simply completing the mission," Allen finished. "I guess they grew tired of trying to grab Bestowen themselves and are forcing us to do it. Sloppy, and the fallout will be ten times worse than it ever would have been if everyone had simply been honest in the first place. Does no one ever look at the whole picture?"

Lace sighed. "I know it doesn't seem like it, but Peter has done everything he can to stop it and minimize the damage, save tell me. That he should have done, and I would have come to you, since I have sense enough to ask for help when a matter has spun out of control." He shot Peter a look that made the man drop his gaze, face twisting with shame. "I am sorry, Your Majesties, High Commander. I should have known, no matter what pains were taken to ensure I didn't. I meant it when I said we had no desire to jeopardize our standing with you. When the Queen hears about all of this, she won't be happy, and a good many people will die."

Sarrica sighed. "That's a mess to be sorted later. Why did Bestowen steal the star? We know for certain he is the responsible party?"

"Yes," Peter said. "He's responsible for arranging the theft. As to why, I don't know; my brother never said."

"That does not sound like Lord Bestowen," Allen said. "He's a merchant, not a politician or thief."

"Everyone has a price," Sarrica replied with a shrug. "Or a secret they don't want getting out. I hope it was worth it, especially if anything else happens to Shemal, because I'm not going to do anything to stop whatever Lesto does with him."

Lesto bent and grabbed Peter's throat again, squeezed hard enough to make breathing impossible. "You had better hope Shemal is alive, or you will learn the hard way that your Blood of the Fallen and the Hands of Death know nothing about being ruthless. I will teach you exactly what it means when we say that the only way to stop an Arseni is to bury us fathoms deep." He let go, left Peter heaving and gasping, and rose. "You will stay here," he said, jabbing a finger at Sarrica and Allen before turning to Rene. "Summon Jader and the Dragons."

"Both of you come home," Sarrica said.

"Try not to lose the other eye," Rene added.

Lesto cast them a parting look of warning then swept from the room in a jangle of armor and sword belt. Once he was in the hallway, he bellowed at the top of his lungs, "Fathoms Deep! All to me!"

Chapter Eight

Shemal's head felt like it had back when he'd been eighteen and exactly as stupid as all people were at that age. He'd just joined his second ship, the first having suffered capture by the Demergo Navy fourteen months into his time aboard. The crew had dared him to drink an entire bottle of Bentan fire whiskey. His head had felt split in half for six days straight, and his stomach hadn't kept down more than gruel for the better part of two weeks.

The crew hadn't stopped laughing for three *months*, but it was still one of the best ships he'd ever sailed on.

Being held captive by gleeful mother fuckers in red leather was a good deal less amusing than a two-week hangover, and he'd *really* hated that hangover.

He tried to shake and wipe away the blood dripping into his right eye, but it was hard to manage when his arms were stretched out and chained to the wall. In the basement of some abandoned building. He assumed it was abandoned, anyway, from the rats and decay and smell of rot.

Shemal knew this play, or at least the raunchier version of it they put on at the kinds of establishments he could afford. He'd been drunk that time as well. The play had ended with a lot of fighting and a paladin wearing remarkably impractical armor swooping in last minute to save her robber lover followed by a half hour victory celebration that had garnered a lot of approval from the drunk, horny audience.

He had really liked that play, but he wasn't stupid enough to think it had anything to do with reality. No one was going to come save him and especially not in such dramatic fashion. Not when, from what little he'd heard and understood, their intention was to trade him for Lord Bestowen. Nobody prioritized an aimless, penniless pirate over a wealthy, powerful noble who served a purpose.

Especially given he'd just broken Lord Tecilia's arm, and apparently had been doing nothing but dragging Lesto down since his arrival.

Shemal tried again to wipe away the blood in his eye, but to no avail. He was lucky the cut on his forehead wasn't worse, but he wasn't feeling terribly grateful right then.

He looked across the basement at the five men sitting around on various broken chairs and old barrels, having some tense conversation that he only caught snatches of. Like any sailor who did it long enough, he knew just enough of several languages to order food, sex, and understand when someone yelled that the authorities were coming. Whatever they were arguing about, it had to do with someone important— a noble or royal, maybe both.

The only light came from a flickering lantern, and there was nothing to ward off the steadily worsening chill.

Mother Ocean, Lesto must be furious with him. Assaulting a noble, running away exactly like he'd promised he wouldn't, and then letting himself get kidnapped—and he hadn't prevented Lord Tara from being hurt in the process. Hopefully, Tara would be all right. He'd looked a little beaten up, but nothing severe. Making certain he got away safe was probably the only thing Shemal had managed to do right.

His eyes stung, a twisting ache stabbing at his chest as he pictured Lesto's face when he found out everything Shemal had done. He'd trusted Shemal, given him so much, and Shemal had stupidly started to believe that maybe something as ridiculous as a pirate loving a duke could actually be possible.

But he had no worthwhile skills when he wasn't on a ship or dealing with stupid goats. He owned nothing but a modest inheritance back home that amounted to a shack and a fishing boat that he'd let his favorite cousin permanently borrow. He could barely read and write. He couldn't provide heirs, which everyone loved to tell him like he was too stupid to know he lacked the necessary parts. Pretending for a moment that Lesto would even want to marry him, if Lesto was adamant about having a blood heir, they would have to get a dame. But the idea made Shemal feel sick and lonely. One of the reasons he'd left home was because he'd just never connected with Islander traditions of poly and open relationships. He wanted one lover who was all his, and most of his family and community had never really understood that.

Not that it mattered when he and Lesto were never going to reach that point together. Shemal's presence was making people doubt Lesto, reconsider contracts, business relationships, court ties... Everyone was thinking less of Lesto because of Shemal, and they were pulling away from him as quickly as possible. If Shemal had done that much damage in just a few days, how much longer would he have lasted? But that didn't really matter either since he'd ruined any chance of holding on to his relationship with Lesto by breaking the arm of that smug, pompous little brat.

And there was no point in worrying about any of it, because he probably wasn't going to be alive come morning.

Why him? That was the part that confounded Shemal the most. He was a pirate who was only involved in the matter by chance—wild, highly improbable chance. He was involved because the two biggest halfwits in the empire had botched a kidnapping and taken Lesto to the one person in all of Gearth who would rather die than ever see him come to harm.

A man who probably hated him now.

Shemal pinched his eyes shut, tried to cling to the happy memories of Lesto. It wasn't fair that one person could affect him so strongly. Two encounters, one violent, one passionate, shouldn't have been enough to carve the man so deeply into his mind.

And if he had thought that was bad, there were no words to describe the havoc Lesto had wreaked in the month and a half that had passed since Lesto had been dropped on his doorstep.

The sound of approaching footsteps drew Shemal from his unhappy thoughts; he opened his eyes and stared at the man who crouched in front of him. The man's mouth curled in a derisive little sneer that Shemal knew all too well, though he didn't understand a word the man said. Dredging up a sneer of his own, he said, *"I don't speak your dirty dog language except to ask how to get the fuck out of your shit country."*

Sneer dropping from his face, the man stood and made to kick him—only to stop when one of the other men barked at him. Shifting to stilted informal Harken, the man said, "With you, I don't see point of the fuss."

"I don't understand why you think pissing off the High Commander and his best friend the High King is a good idea. I thought people preferred to avoid their countries going to war."

Red Leather shrugged. "At the all costs, is my order."

That one took a moment to untangle. "I don't think 'going to war' and 'certain death' are prices I'd be willing to pay." On the other hand, he'd faced exactly that for cargo that proved to be not even half as good as promised. The tattoos mostly hid it, but his body was a legacy of scars acquired fighting for brandy, sugar, spices, and other valuable cargo. He'd seen capture more times than he cared to count and had always survived by luck and the mercy of Mother Ocean.

And the faith of one compelling, breathtaking man who probably never wanted to see him again.

Crouching again, the man prodded at one of his stretched out legs. "You special, why? All this for crime committer?"

"Criminal," Shemal said. "*Pirate, actually.* You'd have to ask Lesto. He's the one who said I'm special. I'm just an Islander with a criminal past."

The man grunted and stood, wandered back over to the others. From the way they kept glancing at him, and the occasional uttering of the word *pirate*, it was clear what they were discussing, but Shemal couldn't begin to guess why.

Maybe they were starting to figure out that he wasn't special enough to make a worthwhile ransom. Hopefully they'd let him go, though Shemal was fairly certain that was not what usually happened to hostages who proved useless.

One of the men abruptly turned and strode off down the long row of the old basement and up the rickety stairs that looked ready to break with every step. Shemal closed his eyes, unable to bear looking at it all, more interested in focusing on all his happy memories of Lesto, no matter how much they hurt.

He opened his eyes again when the man who'd left returned, stomping angrily and managing to crack two of the worn steps. He barked something at the others, who tensed and reached reflexively for their weapons. The leader gestured to Shemal and said something that sounded like an order, but the only familiar word he caught was *move.*

Two of them crossed the room to him, one to each arm as they unchained him and got him up on his shackled feet. Then he was unceremoniously thrown over the larger man's shoulder like a sack of flour. At least they hadn't knocked him out this time. Shemal wasn't certain how much more of a beating his poor head could take. The rough treatment wasn't doing any favors for his other wounds, either, but he preferred the pain to being unconscious.

Though he wished there was a little bit more dignity involved. He considered trying to fight his way free, but he was chained hand and foot, and pirates were only ever that talented in plays. The reality was that he wasn't going anywhere unless his captors let down their guard long enough for him to slip away slowly and get somewhere he could have the manacles removed.

He was dumped over a horse when they reached the streets, the last of the light fading from the sky as they rode off, headed out of the city if the upward slope was anything to judge by. That was stupid. Why would the halfwits venture anywhere close to the Cartha Mountains? Shemal was a *pirate*, and he'd rather face an imperial fleet than deal with the crazy mother fuckers in the mountains.

It took a good day of travel to reach them from Harkenesten, but if they were only halfway there it was still far too close for comfort.

By the time they stopped, it was full dark, miserably cold, and he would give anything for food and something to lessen his pain. That was the other reason he wouldn't be making an escape any time soon—a bad ankle, some severely bruised ribs, the knot on the back of his head, and who knew what else.

Never mind that he officially had no idea where they were, only that he wouldn't be walking back to town unless he had about a week to do it.

They dragged him inside a dilapidated temple, probably abandoned when a newer, better one was built but never torn down because nobody ever thought about that cost when they made such plans. Shemal was forever grateful for the oversight; many an abandoned building had served as hideaway, home, and storage for him over the years.

The way they'd so abruptly left the empty building in the city, the way they'd so quickly left the city, spoke of a plan gone wrong. Whatever consolation Shemal might have taken from that was ruined by the presence of a *lot* of additional soldiers. There was at least a hundred of them milling around the old temple. Worse, they weren't all wearing red leather. A good too fucking many of them wore the uniform of the Hands of Death. Fuck, fuck, and *fuck*.

If that many soldiers were here, even more were

probably close by, likely offshore or divided between buildings, or both. If the same number had been waiting wherever Lesto was supposed to deliver Lord Bestowen... But Lesto was High Commander, he wouldn't do something like that without taking along enforcements, and Fathoms Deep was accounted an unstoppable force, never mind the imperial army.

They'd probably made the red leather brigade think they were bringing Lord Bestowen and then took all of them down. But Lesto had been at the exchange spot, obviously. Only amateur kidnappers would be that foolish, and while he wouldn't accuse the red leather brigade of shining intelligence, they weren't hopelessly stupid either.

Whatever had happened, the rest of the force was pulling back to regroup. They must be keeping Shemal for insurance; he couldn't fathom any other reason, though by now it must have been made clear to them he wasn't worth much.

But far be it for him to tell them if they hadn't already figured it out. Shemal settled without protest as they propped him against what was left of an altar and wrapped his chains around it, securing them at the back, forcing his arms to stretch out again. His shoulders were going to ache for days—assuming he survived the night, which he wasn't.

The five who'd been holding him spoke with a man who had marks of high rank on his shoulders. What rank exactly, Shemal wasn't sure, but it was obvious from the way they all behaved that he was in charge. He was short, the type who always seemed to be bouncing in place even when he was holding perfectly still. He had light skin, dark hair, and a snub nose. Whatever the others were telling him, he wasn't happy about it, and he knocked two of them across the face, sending all of them of scurrying away.

He strode over to Shemal and knelt close to him—but not close enough that Shemal could swing his legs out to kick him, not that he planned on trying. "Your people are quite stupid not to give us the Star when we demanded it."

"What are you talking about?" Shemal asked. "What star? I thought you wanted Lord Bestowen."

"Because he is the one responsible for the theft of our Star. Tell me why Harken is willing to risk war with Treya Mencee for you. What makes you so valuable?"

Shemal snorted. "Tell me why you're willing to start a war with the Harken Empire. The last country to try that was Benta, and they had twice your ability and no ocean in the way. What's so damn important you'd risk everything for it?"

"That is none of your business," the man replied. "Your only concern should be your life, and you will lose it if you do not tell me how to persuade the High Commander to give us what we want."

Laughing, Shemal leaned forward as far as he could, until he and the other man were only a hand span apart, then said in Treyan, *"Suck. My. Dick. You milk-skinned, flea-ridden shit stain."*

That got him backhanded, left his mouth bleeding where his teeth cut the inside of one cheek. Shemal spit blood out as he pulled back to rest against the altar again.

The man glared at him a moment longer then rose and returned to the others.

As victories went, it wasn't much, and Shemal was definitely going to pay for it later by way of a slow death. But he was always going to die anyway, and he'd be damned to the depths before he betrayed Lesto when it mattered most. Bad enough he'd already fucked up so irrevocably.

He looked up as the man he'd spoken to suddenly got loud, just in time to see him shove several of the men away. Maybe he'd be so busy killing his own people he'd forget to kill Shemal.

Some other men got into it, and the argument quickly turned into shoving and shouting. A few more minutes and somebody was going to throw a punch, and that would be that. Looked like it was going to be Red Leather versus the Hands of Death. Shemal was going to put his non-existent money on the Hands of Death. Red Leather didn't seem tough or scary. Ten of them hadn't been able to stop Shemal and Lesto in the end.

He refused to think about how much of that had been dumb luck.

Right as the whole fight was about to turn nasty, something came through one of the temple windows—a fire arrow. It was followed immediately by several more, plunging into the temple, striking stone and men, turning everything to chaos.

Before the mercenaries could recover, the doors were thrown open and soldiers surged in, all wearing the unmistakable teal of Fathoms Deep. Shemal swallowed, throat suddenly raw. What was Fathoms Deep doing there? They shouldn't—

All his thoughts stuttered to a halt as Lesto came storming through the broken door. Instead of his usual uniform and lightweight leather armor, he wore chain mail, plate guards on his arms and legs, heavy gauntlets on his hands, and over all that was a Fathoms Deep surcoat, the skull and swords crest emblazoned in black and silver thread. With the patch over his eye, the drawn sword, the brutal way he fought as he joined the fray... Lesto looked more like a pirate than a soldier. Shemal couldn't have looked away even if he'd wanted to. Lesto was fierce and beautiful, but at the same time, he was safe and stable, so very much a port in a storm.

Three men broke away from other fights to attack him, but Lesto threw a gauntleted fist into the face of the first, countered the swinging sword of the next with his own, tripped the third one, and then finished off the second. By the time he was done with that, the first one had recovered enough to find somewhere else to be.

Lesto took down several more mercs as he fought his way across the room, fighting with all the ruthlessness of a pirate—a pirate captain, determined to plunder and keep as many of his crew alive as possible.

He was halfway down the hall when he saw Shemal and stopped in surprise—a move that nearly cost him, as two men came at him from behind. Shemal jerked reflexively at his chains. "Behind!"

Whipping around, Lesto drew a dagger from his belt, disarmed one man while kicking away the other then killing both of them, one with a sword to his gut, the other with a dagger to his throat. Retrieving the sword the second man dropped, he continued on with two blades until he at last reached the altar.

By that point, the fighting was winding down and any remaining enemies had been secured. Lesto looked cautiously around before kneeling beside Shemal. "Someone find me keys or a close approximation!" Lesto bellowed. He dropped his swords, stripped off the heavy gauntlets, and touched Shemal's face. "Are you all right?"

"What are you doing here?" Shemal asked. "Where's Bestowen?"

"What?" Lesto stared at him, hand falling. "What are you talking about? What do you mean what am I doing here? People are usually a little happier than this when they're rescued."

Shemal stared back. "You shouldn't be here. I don't understand."

"Why do you keep asking that like I wouldn't come for you?" Lesto withdrew. "We'll talk about this later. Are you all right, other than your obviously addled head?"

"My head isn't addled, you enthusiastic mother fucking—"

Lesto's mouth twisted. "You can't be feeling too awful if you're back to declaring I particularly enjoy fucking my mother, though you could bother to look happy to see me." A guard came running up before he could say more and vanished behind the altar after examining the chains briefly.

A few minutes later, Shemal's arms were free. He groaned as he tried to work the stiffness and pain from his abused shoulders.

"Are you all right?" Lesto asked again, voice softer, expression concerned and confused as he looked Shemal over.

Shemal nodded. "Been worse. Could use some rest." He stared at Lesto, at a loss. Why wasn't he angry? Where was Bestowen? "I still don't understand what's going on or why you're here. What about Bestowen? The star they keep mentioning?"

Lesto's face hardened. "You don't have to keep

looking so damned surprised that I came for you. At the very least, you could have expected me to return a damned favor. Gratifying to know your real opinion of me." Before Shemal could say anything, he rose and started calling out to his men, bringing officers running to report.

Watching Lesto do what he did best was more enthralling than it had any right to be, especially when Shemal couldn't even explain what had just happened. He'd expected Lesto to be angry with him... then Lesto had shown up... and not been angry with him until Shemal *made* him angry.

Life was a good deal less confounding when Lesto wasn't in it.

A pair of soldiers approached him before he could go after Lesto and bid Shemal follow them outside to a waiting horse. Why it took two of them to say that, Shemal couldn't begin to guess and didn't care enough to ask. He limped after them, one hand curled protectively over the spot where his ribs ached the most.

When they reached the horse, he stared at it as exhaustion washed over him. "I'm not sure I can climb on that. Where's Lesto?"

"Commander's up there, sorting out the prisoners," one of them said. "We can help you up, or we can get a cart if you prefer. Think there's one about."

Shemal shook his head. No way was he riding in a cart like a child or a whiny noble. "Help me on the horse, and we'll just have to hope I can stay on it."

Mounting the horse took far more effort than it should have, and pretty much every part of his body hated him for it, but he did at last manage it. He thanked the soldiers, who smiled, sketched slight bows, and strode briskly off to their own horses.

Looking toward Lesto, Shemal hesitated. Could he ride over there? Should he stay back?

He startled when Lesto's gaze abruptly turned to him, caught his eyes. Shemal froze, not able to look away but not sure if he should stare either. Damn it, he wanted Lesto. To be close to him. To see him happy. Why was Lesto mad at him for all the wrong things?

Lesto looked away, resumed speaking to the rather ominous-looking woman at his side, and the fragile hope Shemal hadn't realized existed withered and died. It shouldn't matter. He'd spent every second of his captivity convinced Lesto hated him. What did it matter if it was for a different reason? The end result was the same.

A relationship between a powerful, respected lord and a criminal had always been doomed to sink. Shemal should be grateful it had ended with so little fuss. He could have been thrown out, arrested, mysteriously vanished...

The two soldiers from before rejoined him, one on either side, and Shemal had little choice but to fall into step as they rode back to the palace. More than once, he considered just riding off, but he was exhausted and in far too much pain to get very far. And like so many other occasions, more than he cared to count, he had not a pence to his name. What little money he'd had on him when he'd been kidnapped had been taken by his captors.

He'd grit his teeth and get through the night in the palace, then leave in the morning when he was better rested and would have the energy to travel and earn some coin. He doubted he could convince any ship to take him, but there were always merchant companies traveling the continent who would hire him on as cheap labor.

Damn it, he'd like the idea of settling down with Lesto, being his scandalous lover, becoming friends with High Consort Allen and Lord Tara.

It wasn't fair that something so hard to reach was so easily snatched away.

He'd been better off with the goats and wishful thinking.

By the time they reached the palace, his vision was blurry and every step was a little wobbly. He let the poor soldiers assigned to be his babysitters haul him through the palace to what turned out to be the healing ward. They dropped him on a cot, and moments later, Shemal was asleep.

He woke to the chatter and bustle of the healing ward, groggy and stiff, but better than he'd felt when he'd fallen asleep.

A woman in a healer's jacket stopped as she saw him. "Good morning! How are you feeling?" She walked over to him and briskly went about checking him over. "You look much better than when they brought you in. You were pretty bruised, a few cuts and scrapes, but as long as you mind those ribs, you should be fine in a few days."

"That's good hearing," Shemal managed. "Um. Has anyone been by? Is there somewhere I should be?" She shook her head, and disappointment dropped like a stone into Shemal's stomach. Part of his mind tried to point out that Treya Mencee had practically declared war on Harken, so Lesto was probably busy helping to sort out the mess.

The rest of his mind wouldn't listen, not when

Lesto had been so cold and angry. Not when it was obvious Shemal had done something wrong that couldn't be fixed.

"Guess I should be getting on with the day, then," Shemal said, mustering a smile he definitely didn't feel. "Thank you for tending me." He climbed off the cot, ignoring her protestations to rest a little longer, and slowly walked away.

Out of the healing ward, he looked around in confusion and picked a random hallway. It took him nearly ten minutes of walking before he found an area that looked familiar. From there, he was finally able to make it back to Lesto's suite, and thankfully, the guards let him past and the door wasn't locked.

The urge to curl up in Lesto's bed, lose himself in the comfort and memories it brought to mind, was so powerful that resisting was a physical ache. But Mother Ocean, how angry would Lesto be to find him there acting like he still had every right?

Shemal closed his eyes and stood still, until he was able to shove everything back enough to function. Opening his eyes, he drew a ragged breath, then crossed the bedroom to the dressing room. After a few minutes of searching, he found his old clothes packed away in the very back with some other items clearly kept more for sentiment than need. Discarding the ones he wore, he pulled on the slightly oversized clothes he'd borrowed from the garrison. Still not his own, but those were long gone. He'd be able to afford something more suitable once he found work and earned a bit of coin. Lesto would probably never notice if he took some money from the case he kept in the dressing room, but just the idea of doing that turned Shemal's stomach.

Returning to the main room, he looked around for something to write a note, his gaze finally falling on the writing desk in the corner. Going over to it, he sat down and slowly, painfully, wrote out his farewell in awkward, clumsy Harken. He cringed looking it over, like something written by a bumbling child, nothing at all like the pretty script on the letters and other papers stacked neatly on the desk. One more humiliating reminder that thinking he and Lesto would ever work had been a fool's wish. He hesitated a moment, then wrote out the same words in Islander, just in case his Harken was as shitty as he feared. Not that his Islander was much better, his little corner of the world had little use for such things.

Now, where best to leave the note? He wandered around the suite, considering his options, lingered in the bedroom where he finally settled on Lesto's bureau, on top of his jewelry case. He folded it in half and left it propped, stared at it as second thoughts and foolish ideas spun around in his head like a whirlpool trying to drag him under.

In the end, he resisted, though only by focusing on how humiliating it would be to find Lesto only to be cut down and thrown out in front of all the people perpetually surrounding Lesto. Including the man whose arm he'd broken, likely poised to gloat as Shemal got what he deserved.

Come to that, he was surprised no one had been waiting by his bed to arrest him.

Not that he was complaining. He'd find some labor in the city, earn a bit of coin, then find cheap passage out of the city and be on his way to the border by end of day tomorrow. In a few weeks, he'd be back in Gearth and hunting down his poor, neglected goats.

Life would be back to dreary, boring normal, and maybe he could finally put away hopeless dreams of the man who would always be out of reach.

Getting out of the palace was easy enough, almost depressingly so. He both hoped and dreaded that someone would call his name, come rushing to stop him. Beg him not to go. Ha. His own family hadn't begged him to stay when he'd said he was leaving. None of his friends had asked him to stay, or tried to go with him when he'd said he was quitting the pirate life. Why in the world would anyone else? He hunched his shoulders as he passed through the main gates and folded into the general throng of people leaving the palace. When they were clear of it, he edged away from the crowd, more comfortable with space around him. His ribs ached, but he ignored the pain as best he could and tried to think of places that were likely to offer work so late in the day with no questions asked.

He was standing in line to pass through the city gates when he heard the crowd stirring, followed almost immediately by the thundering of a horse underscored by a familiar jangling. But that made no sense, and really, Lesto wasn't the only soldier who jangled. Rolling his eyes at himself, Shemal turned to see what had the crowd whispering and exclaiming— and froze as he saw Lesto pounding down the line, his eyes sweeping the crowd.

Lesto stilled as their gazes collided, face darkening like storm clouds overtaking a clear sky. Riding over to Shemal, he said, "I knew I should have set guards to watch over you. Get on the damned horse."

"But—"

"Shut up and get on the damned horse, or I will throw you over this saddle," Lesto said. *"Now."*

167

Apparently he wasn't going to be allowed to leave quietly and without fuss. Shemal stepped out of line, took the hand Lesto offered, and swung up behind him on the horse. Before he could even draw breath to ask a question, Lesto had heeled the horse into motion again, and they were riding off far too quickly for speaking to be possible.

They also weren't heading back to the palace. Shemal rested his head between Lesto's shoulders to keep the road dust out of his eyes and waited miserably to find out what was going on.

CHAPTER NINE

It was the dead of night when they reached Fathoms Deep, though they'd stopped only for necessary breaks and to obtain fresh horses. Lesto could barely see straight by the time he dismounted. The door flew open and two of his footmen came rushing out just as another figure came from around the house to take the horses.

"Your Grace, welcome home," one of the footmen said. "Do you need me to take anything?"

"No, thank you," Lesto replied. "We would like something to eat in my sitting room. Tell the chef something quick and light is fine. I'd like my bedroom prepared as well, please. No additional room. Lord Shemal will be staying with me. Introductions can wait until another day. We're not to be disturbed until I say otherwise."

"Yes, Your Grace," the footmen chorused and vanished into the house to dispense his orders.

Lesto turned to Shemal, stopped as he saw the way Shemal stared at his home. Not with greed or approval or feigned disinterest, but awe. Lesto's stomach clenched, mind replaying for the thousandth time how it had felt to walk into his bedroom in search of Shemal, worried after the healers had reported he'd left looking distraught, to find nothing but a note.

A note that had made him feel even more horrible than he already had. It had obviously been written with care, but Lesto had still been forced to find Allen to make sense of it, and hearing the words had felt like someone had torn his chest open. *You were my port. I'm sorry I ruined everything.*

He stepped closer, reached out—and flinched slightly when Shemal tensed, dropped his gaze to stare at Lesto, and then stared at the ground as he muttered, "Sorry, I didn't mean to gawk like a halfwit."

"You weren't," Lesto said gruffly. "It's my home. I want you to like it."

Shemal opened his mouth, closed it, stared at him like he had no idea what he was looking at. Lesto tried not to wince. "I don't understand why I'm here."

"Because I keep hoping it will be your home, too," Lesto replied. "Come on, I'm hungry." He strode off, hoping if he kept moving forward with little chance for argument Shemal would keep following him.

Inside, Shemal muttered something in Farland, and when Lesto turned to look at him, he was once again staring around in awe. Even Lesto was still impressed with the entryway: all white stone threaded with veins of gold that led up to the stained glass roof of a white and black compass surrounded by teal. It mirrored the very same on the floor. At the far end was the long, wide, winding staircase that split in two directions at the first landing, leading to three doors of dark wood and more stained glass which led to the west, north, and east wings of the manor. The doors were exactly in line with those below that led to the downstairs portions of the same, save the middle door, which led to the public rooms of the house and eventually the servant quarters. The second floor landing wrapped all the way around the hall, the area over the entrance leading to a balcony that overlooked the whole front of the manor and the road leading to it, the fields and work buildings off in the distance.

"Do you like it?"

"It's beautiful," Shemal replied, looking at him briefly before shyly glancing away again. "It's as stunning as the palace without being quite as intimidating. Though it's still far too much for a pirate." His gaze dropped unhappily to the floor.

Lesto's mouth tightened. Food and rest would have to wait. "Come with me."

Shemal gave a soft huff, mouth curving ever so briefly in a familiar smile—but it collapsed in the next moment. Lesto hated seeing Shemal so wary, but he had only himself to blame for ruining the easiness between them. Hopefully he would be able to recover it.

He led Shemal through the door on the left, into the depths of the lower west wing, down all the way to the end to a large, heavy metal door. Where the lock should have been was instead a large, round dial. "Do you remember when I said I wanted to tell you about the coordinates?"

"It would be hard to forget, given you nearly died," Shemal said. "That aside, I can count on one hand the number of people who have said they trust me, and only one of them was a High Commander."

Lesto smiled briefly. "They're not actually coordinates. My family has long used sailing coordinates to write in code, and teaching you the code is part of 'telling you about the coordinates.' But the ones on my ring, on the full crest, are the secret to getting into this room. Though only the family knows the correct order." He turned the dial to the first number, then the next, going through thirteen numbers in all before the door gave a muted click.

Lesto pulled open the door, motioned for Shemal to precede him, and pulled the door shut behind them.

Lesto walked across the room with familiar ease, lit the lamp he knew was on the shelf directly across from the door, and used its light to see by as he lit the rest. When he was done, he motioned for Shemal to join him in the middle of the room.

"What is this place?" Shemal asked quietly. The floor was made of dark and light stained wood that formed the crest of Fathoms Deep. It was large enough to show the one detail the smaller versions had to leave out: the compass in the right eye was framed by a circle of coordinates, the same ones wrapped around the outer edge of his signet.

Around the rest of the circular room was shelves filled with books: journals, diaries, memoirs, sketchbooks, manuals, and volumes of art done by the Arseni family, as well as history books. A single space was left open in the walls of shelves, filled with the original teal flag with the Fathoms Deep crest, set in a frame made from the wood of the last ship the first Duchess had sailed. Around the top of the wall was carved the family motto, and the ceiling was made of light and dark wood shaped into a compass.

Lesto smiled proudly. "We call it the memory vault, except for Rene, who likes to call it the mausoleum."

Shemal winced slightly. "What's a mausoleum?"

"A tomb for multiple people," Lesto replied. "Rene tends toward the morbid."

"I can see where he'd get it, if this place stores memories," Shemal said. "Memory and memorial are pretty close."

Lesto laughed softly. "Fair point, but I'm not telling Rene that. Anyway, the point is that this is a place for family. Access to this room grants access to full knowledge of our family. All the good, great, bad, and terrible. Secrets that could be used against us. Secrets that could be used to hurt others. Only those the Arseni consider family are allowed in here. We aren't allowed to share the secret without the approval of the rest of the family—approval Rene, Tara, Sarrica, and Allen didn't hesitate to grant. Currently, they, you, and I are the only ones with access."

Shemal looked around the room again, mouth opening and closing several times before he finally looked back at Lesto and said roughly, "You were so angry and cold, and I know I was a burden, never mind I assaulted a noble and broke his arm. I thought you'd decided you were better off without me."

"I didn't mean to be cold; I was hurt you weren't happy to see me when I came to rescue you. I should have listened better, had more patience. As to that little rat who harassed you—he and his family have been banned and fined, and if he's smart, he'll stay out of our sight for a very long time," Lesto replied, angry all over again at the vindictive little bastard's gall. "You've never been a burden. Why would you think that?"

Shemal's mouth twisted and he looked away again, heavy dreads spilling over his shoulders. "I generally have no problem ignoring people when they voice a low opinion of me, but it's harder to ignore when they speak of withdrawing support and friendship and loyalty because they feel they can't trust a man who would take up with someone like me."

"Chances are I never liked any of them anyway," Lesto replied. "Even if I did, if they're so fickle then I'm just as happy to know it and be rid of them. The only thing that has ever bothered me is that you thought I wouldn't come to save you."

"Couldn't," Shemal said. "I thought you *couldn't* come to save me. I couldn't understand everything they said, but it seemed clear they wanted to trade me for Bestowen. There is no choice between a lord with people depending on him, a man of wealth and power who was needed and would be missed, and a penniless, faceless pirate no one would ever notice was missing."

"It occurred to me later that might be your thinking—damn near too late because by the time I was finally able to get away from the damned arguments with Treya Mencee to come see you, it was to be told you'd left. I went to our room hoping you were there..." He sighed. "I nearly set guards to watch you, but I thought you'd be fine in the healing ward, and I would have time to come see you."

Shemal's eyes brightened slightly. "You were going to come see me?"

"Yes, but as seems to be your habit, you'd already run away," Lesto said.

Shemal ducked his head, cheeks darkening. "I didn't mean to the first time, after I broke that man's arm. I panicked, was afraid they'd punish you for my behavior. Later, after I woke up in the healing ward, I figured everyone would be happier if I left without fuss. I didn't *want* to leave."

Some of the remaining knots in Lesto's chest started to loosen. He closed the space between them, spanned his hands across Shemal's stomach, and leaned in to kiss him. That made him feel better than he had since learning Shemal had been kidnapped.

More knots loosened and fell away as he kissed Shemal slowly, lapping at his lips, pressing deeper briefly, drawing back to do it all over again, savoring the feel and flavor, sinking into the rightness of having him so close. "I didn't want you to leave either."

"S-so I'm gathering," Shemal said softly, a touch of breathlessness in his voice. "Unless there's a strange tradition of dragging pirates to your estate to use in some arcane ceremony."

Lesto laughed. "No, I have much more interesting reasons to drag you to my estate. But speaking of pirates, that *is* one of the other reasons I brought you here." He brushed another kiss across Shemal's mouth, then drew back and motioned to where the family motto was carved all around the top edge of the walls. *We Will Stop Only When You Bury Us Fathoms Deep.* "Farther back than most historical accounts bother to go, the Harkenos family was not even royalty, only a tattered noble house trying to save what was left of the royal family. When they died, the Harkenos assumed the role, far more reluctantly than anyone likes to recall. They became the fragile new rulers of a kingdom struggling against their many enemies on land, and fighting to keep what little wealth they possessed from pirates.

"There was one pirate in particular they could not defeat, a woman named Stalia Arseni, who was well known for saying that the only way to stop her was to bury her fathoms deep. It's a long story, but the short version is that she and Mattica Harkenos became fast friends and when he asked for her support, she gave it. The kingdom of Harken was saved because of their friendship, and Stalia became the first Duchess of Fathoms Deep. The mercenaries were founded a couple of generations later, when Harken was dragged into war again and a kingdom started to become an empire."

Turning to face Shemal, who gaped at him with mouth open, Lesto added, "The obvious point of all of this being that anyone who says a pirate is not worthy of Fathoms Deep is a fool. You belong here more than anyone else could."

Shemal kissed him, hard and fierce, fingers cupping his face, warm and calloused, so familiar and right it left an ache.

Lesto returned the kiss, until his lips were sore and they were both panting. "Are you done running away now, you stupid pirate?"

"I'm not opposed to a bit more convincing," Shemal replied and kissed him again, pushing Lesto back until he struck the door. "I didn't think I'd get to do this anymore."

Lesto's mouth quirked. "You'll get to do it plenty, believe me. But first, I think we need food and rest, as I'm sure you're even more worn out than me."

Sighing softly, Shemal drew back. "You might have a point, especially with the way my ribs still hurt, but I concede it with ill grace."

"Noted," Lesto said with a laugh. "Come on." He paused to take a blue velvet bag from a drawer and slide it into a pocket, then opened the door and waited until Shemal was in the hall before extinguishing the lamps and locking the door. "I'll give you a tour of the rest of the place tomorrow. It's mostly the original that was built forever ago, but some parts were destroyed by fire a century ago and had to be rebuilt. And little things are always changing as needs and preferences shift." Back in the main entry, he went up the stairs and down a hall in the east wing, through a door that was mostly red stained glass into his private sitting room.

The room was comprised of two long, deep sofas of black leather, red and gray rugs on the dark wooden floor, other splashes of red, gray, and silver scattered about, including heavy red drapes left open to display the stained glass window of red roses and dark green vines.

"This room looks like you," Shemal said quietly, looking around.

"I hope that's a good thing," Lesto said as he sat on one of the sofas and pulled the covers off the trays of food. Despite his order for something simple, the chef had sent along steaming soup, warmed bread with herb butter, and a platter of cheese and fruit. There was also a pitcher of beer, probably one of those his recently-acquired brewers had been working on. He looked up when Shemal's silence stretched on, saw the sheepish look on his face. "So it is a good thing?"

"I... back when I first woke up in your room at Harkenesten Palace, I admired all your jewelry, wondered if you ever actually wore any of it. You wear teal well, but I always thought you'd look even better in black pearls and rubies." The flush that washed over his skin made it fairly easy to guess what else had been in those thoughts.

Lesto smiled, maybe inwardly preening a bit that Shemal thought about what he'd look good in and clearly wanted to see if he was right. "As it happens, I'm rather fond of black pearls, I have a couple of pieces that include rubies, and I do wear them on occasion—especially when persuaded to by pirates making filthy promises. Come sit down and eat."

Shemal shot him a grin as he trailed around the room instead, touching the drapes, the window, the books on the shelves in one corner. "Is that all it takes? How convenient that I'm a pirate capable of making and fulfilling a good many filthy promises." He paused in front of a painting of Lesto, Nyle, and Rene as little boys. "You look like you were a troublesome child."

"Hardly. Who had time to get into trouble when I was forever trying to get those two out of it? That painting was right before Nyle left to live with some friends of my mother. He was sick for a long time. They thought a different atmosphere would help him. As it turned out, they were right. He returned hale and hearty and wound up marrying Sarrica." Lesto smiled sadly.

"I'm sorry he died," Shemal said and finally came to sit next to him. "That smells amazing."

Lesto's sadness fell back as he laughed. "Yes, I am looking forward to being here more. The food at Harken is nothing to sneer at, but there's something to be said for the food I grew up on."

They lapsed into silence as they ate, and both were yawning by the time they'd finished off every last bite and drop. Shemal sat back with a groan. "I am getting entirely too used to eating like a spoiled lord."

"Oh, so food is the secret to keeping you where I want you, hmm?" Lesto asked, leaning back to rest against Shemal's side, propping one foot on the sofa. If Shemal was troubled by taking all his weight, he gave no sign of it. Instead, he shifted slightly so he could wrap an arm loosely around Lesto. "What foods in particular?"

"Not fish," Shemal muttered. "Just one of many reasons I'm something of a disgrace back home, but I really hate fish."

Lesto laughed hard enough he nearly upset his balance, though he wasn't terribly sorry when it ended with them both on the couch, him using Shemal as a pillow, nestled between those large, heavy thighs. After the past couple of days, it was the best possible improvement. The fingers running over his close-cut hair weren't bad, either. "If this is what my life will be like when I'm no longer High Commander, I may send Sarrica my retirement tomorrow."

"It's never going to stop being disconcerting that you say the High King's name so casually," Shemal said.

"You'll do it, too, eventually," Lesto replied with a laugh. He closed his eye, exhaustion washing back over him in the wake of all that food and the warm comfort of lying against Shemal.

After a few minutes the caressing ceased. "If you're going to fall asleep on me, I'd much rather it be in a bed."

Lesto reluctantly sat up. "I suppose that's a fair point, and I am damned fond of my bed here." He stood and offered a hand. "Come on." Holding fast, he led the way down a couple of hallways to where the family bedrooms were located, including the master suite he'd taken over several months after his parents died. At the time, he'd been content to stay in his old room, but the servants did as they pleased while he was gone, and it had pleased them to put their new lord where they thought he belonged.

He hadn't minded in the end because the master suite was luxurious enough almost to shame the High Palace. His servants, as flawless and wonderful as always, had left lamps burning in the front room, which was decorated in various shades of blue, the ceiling done in blocks of frosted colored glass, lending the whole place a lazy, almost underwater feel. Colorful rugs were scattered on the gold-toned wooden floor, furniture stained the same, all the blue cut with accents of white and sandy gold.

The suite contained the front room, a private sitting room, a private library, the bedroom, and a door that led to the nursery. Lesto turned away from it, headed for the bedroom, and threw the door open. Shemal came up behind him, drew a startled breath, muttered in Farlander before saying in Harken, "Stunning."

"Yes, the architects and designers of long ago outdid themselves." Unlike most beds in Harken, which were freestanding so they could be moved about, his bed was built into the wall. It was bigger than his bed in Harken, and required some effort to climb in and out of—and was well worth the effort. The front was framed by more colored glass depicting ships at sea. There was also a set of steps leading up to the bed as well as a small table where books and tea and such were often left. Curtains could be pulled from the other side, the only light from still more blocks of frosted glass that lined the top of the walls surrounding the bed.

His servants had laid a fire and left plenty of water in two large washbasins. Lesto stripped, leaving his sword belt hanging off the back of a chair at the table near the fire. His clothes he threw in a basket meant for that purpose. Pausing only to grab a rag and soap, he knelt in one of the basins and quickly scrubbed himself clean. A proper bath was in order for the morrow, but right then, a scrub down was more than adequate.

When he was finished, leaving Shemal to his own washing, Lesto strode into the dressing chamber and pulled down two drying cloths and two robes. The robes he left on hooks in the wall off to one side of the bed before returning to Shemal with the drying clothes. He dried himself off with one, watched with impatience and pleasure as Shemal finished washing and stood, water sluicing down his colorful, toned body.

Shemal stepped out of the basin, accepted the cloth Lesto held out, and quickly dried off. When he was done, Lesto reeled him and dropped a firm kiss on his mouth. "As much as I would love to savor every scrap of your naked body, I am far too tired."

"Old man," Shemal said with a chuckle. "Not that I'm any better. I really want to try out that bed."

"Then let's do that," Lesto said and dragged him over and into it, smiling at Shemal's gasp as he saw the inside, where moonlight spilled down from small, staggered squares of clear glass in the peaked roof. "The memory vault is directly below here, part of the large tower in this corner of the manor. There are four in all, and five smaller turrets."

"Can't have a proper manor without showy towers and turrets," Shemal drawled, and laughed when Lesto jabbed him. He finally flopped down on the bed, sprawled out, hair covering most of the pillow, and moaned. "I'm never leaving this bed."

"You'll have to eventually," Lesto said, not without sympathy. "Some foods can't be eaten in bed."

Shemal grumbled in Farlander, but sounded too cheerful to be truly bothered.

Shifting closer, Lesto curled against Shemal's side as had quickly become a habit over their few days

181

together in the palace. Coming home had never felt so much like coming home.

"Is Lord Tara all right?" Shemal asked, voice already growing heavy with sleep. "I kept meaning to ask."

"Thanks to you, he's fine, and being spoiled to death by Rene," Lesto said, not bothering to open his eye. "I'll tell you the whole mess with Treya Mencee tomorrow."

Shemal's fingers trailed lazily along his skin, warm and soothing, and within minutes, Lesto was fast asleep.

~~*

He woke to the clatter of dishes, the smell of breakfast, and the murmur of quiet conversation. That definitely wasn't in Harken. Throwing back the blankets, briefly disappointed there was no naked pirate to thoroughly enjoy, Lesto crawled to the entrance and climbed out.

"Good morning, Your Grace!" Leeta, his personal servant, walked over to the dressing robe still hanging on its hook and held it out for him. He shrugged into it, thanked her, and wandered over to where Shemal was already eating breakfast and talking at rapid-fire pace with the servants who'd brought the food. One Farlander, the other half-Farlander, half-Gearthish.

Lesto sat and poured a cup of tea, sighed at the stack of papers that had already appeared—including two sealed envelopes with his name written in Sarrica's familiar brisk, impatient scrawl. May as well get it over with, though if Sarrica was interrupting his break before it could even truly begin, he wasn't going to like what Lesto did to him when he returned to the palace.

He drank a few swallows of tea, took a bite of cinnamon pastry, then used the letter opener set with the stack of correspondence to slit the wax seal and unfold the first letter. He read it quickly. "Lord Bestowen has finally come clean about his involvement: his businesses are not doing as well as he's been making everyone think, and when he was paid large sums of money to arrange the theft of a 'Treyan trinket', he was happy to take it. Given private mercenaries of the sort he hires are very strongly about taking money and not asking questions..." Lesto set the letter aside.

"Whatever happened to the star they kept asking me about?"

"The Star of Menceera was given to Sarrica by Bestowen, and it will remain locked in the imperial vault until Sarrica feels like returning it to Treya Mencee."

Shemal laughed. "So never then."

"More or less," Lesto said with a smirk. "Sarrica's new favorite hobby is sitting back and watching Allen bend everyone to his will. Allen likes a challenge, Treya Mencee is being difficult—Sarrica is having more fun than anyone should under such circumstances. Treya Mencee will get their Star back when Allen gets everything he wants, and given all the deaths and harm Treya Mencee has caused... Well, a kinder man than me might feel bad for them."

"They don't deserve kindness."

"Agreed." Lesto took another bite of pastry and opened the second envelope from Sarrica.

I've announced your retirement. Jader isn't comfortable bossing me around yet, but I feel he'll measure up before the month is out. Return at your leisure. Allen is having fun planning your wedding present when he's not busy terrorizing Treya Mencee. If you take too long, I fear he and Tara will also plan the wedding; they're already discussing ideas. ~S

Lesto mentally drafted a scathing reply as he refilled his teacup and ate the rest of his pastry.

"You look ready to kill someone," Shemal said. "Or at least severely maim them. Is something else wrong?"

"No. Sarrica is being bossy and obnoxious as usual." Lesto selected another pastry, this one piled with soft bits of spiced fruits and creamy cheese. "I said I was returning home for a week or two but would be back. He's informed me he announced my retirement and I should stay here as long as I like."

Shemal laughed, turned briefly to bid farewell to the servants as they slipped away, then turned back to Lesto. "How do a bossy man and a controlling man work so well together? Will it be hard, not being commander and always helping him?"

"Undoubtedly, but I'm sure I'll wind up helping him in other ways," Lesto said with a shrug. He and Sarrica were used to being in one another's space, and it didn't feel right when they operated entirely apart, though they both had plenty of duties that required it. He took a sip of tea. "Speaking of Treya Mencee and trouble, that is a mess that will take some time to sort out and I am glad I need have no further part in it. Sarrica and Allen are doing their best to avoid war, but however it ends, you can bet Treya Mencee will be no friend of ours for quite some time. The original crime was Bestowen's, and he's being punished for it, but Treya Mencee's behavior far outstripped the crime. Normally, someone like myself or Lord Tara would be sent to Treya Mencee to discuss the matter with the queen in person, but Allen and Sarrica fear we'd only wind up murdered in our beds, and I can't say their suppositions are wrong. So right now they are weighing their options, trying to pick a noble they can trust to do the job but who is not so powerful he'd be worth killing to make a point."

"That sounds even less thrilling than deciding if we should face down heavily armed mercenaries or the imperial army," Shemal replied.

Lesto cast him an amused look. "All I care is that the matter is over where I am concerned, and the rest is on people paid to fix such problems. Does the choice of mercenary or army come up often?"

"More often than you'd think." Shemal grinned. "I usually went with imperial army. They tend to obey their own rules, at least when it's not just Islanders in the mix. Mercenaries tend to do whatever is most profitable, whether it's against the rules or not. Though to be fair, I think mercenaries are hired because they don't have much respect for rules."

"Essentially," Lesto replied. "I'm glad my army isn't completely reprehensible. I try to make them all too terrified to disobey me, but there's a lot of people and very little time."

"Oh, everyone knows of High Commander Lesto and the folly of incurring his wrath." Shemal's smile softened, eyes sliding away as he focused on a memory. "The rumors do not do the reality justice."

Lesto snorted. "The reality where I told the lot of you to stop being rowdy, and you accused me of fucking my mother and gave me a black eye? Yes, I can tell you were quite overcome by the sight of me." He started to laugh, but the sudden flush to Shemal's cheeks drew him up short. "You cannot tell me you were anything but derisive."

"Intimidated, maybe," Shemal said. "Mostly in awe. I'm not sure you're aware of the way people calm down around you. What we call a—" He said the words in Farlander, then frowned and said it again in Harken. "Storm tamer."

"I'm pretty certain I'm not," Lesto replied, holding his teacup more tightly because even he knew how important that term was to Farlanders. Jader had spoken of the term before with no small reverence in his voice. It was a title applied to elders and highly respected leaders. He set his teacup down. "You said I was your port."

Shemal's cheeks darkened again, but he didn't look away that time. "Yes. You're calming... safe... and I have always been very good at wandering and running and causing trouble wherever I go. You were able to read my note, then?" He dropped his eyes, fork restlessly moving around the remaining food on his plate. "I wasn't certain... Well, it's obvious I'm no lord trained to read and write."

"I read it fine," Lesto said, because he'd rather die right that very moment than make Shemal feel even more ashamed of himself. "If you're looking for something to occupy your time, and you really want to write in all the ridiculous loops and curves of a spoiled noble, finding a tutor would be a simple matter. Please do, then I can foist some of my work upon you."

Looking up slowly, Shemal smiled hesitantly. "I'm sorry—"

"Oh, don't apologize. I'm sorry I've probably done things that made you feel worse about it. I should know better, but a spoiled brat is a spoiled brat even when they try their hardest not to be." He shrugged. "Reading and writing can be taught. Integrity and heart cannot, and those you have enough of to fill an ocean."

Shemal's smile turned into a full-fledged grin. "If you're hoping flattery will lead to fucking, you're on the right course."

Lesto glanced at the rest of the pile of work awaiting his attention. None of it had been marked as urgent... and beneath all of it was a small, narrow wooden box and the velvet pouch he'd taken from the vault. There was a note affixed to the box from his steward. *We were going to send these off to the palace this morning. ~G*

He smiled faintly. "As delightful as the idea of going back to bed sounds, I have a couple of gifts for you first."

"Gifts?" Shemal asked, dropping his fork on his plate and wiping his mouth with a napkin. "You've already given me, well, everything. I don't have anything—"

"Oh, stop it," Lesto cut in as he stood, picking up the pouch and box. "If it helps any, these are mostly necessary items if you're going to keep putting up with me. Come here."

Shemal pushed away from the table, stood, and joined him. He took the pouch as Lesto held it out, opened it, and tipped the contents into his hand—a ring of keys similar to Lesto's. "What are these?"

"Keys to the estate, the offices and warehouses on the property, and various rooms back at the palace. Rene and Tara have similar sets. These particular keys once belong to Nyle."

"I can't—"

"They were sitting in the vault collecting dust," Lesto said and handed him the box. "These I did not expect to be ready so soon, but my staff is nothing if not impeccable."

Shemal stared at the box, ran his fingers over the top, where a Harken schooner in full glory had been carved.

Lesto shoved lightly at his shoulder. "Open it, already."

"I wish you'd stop giving me things," Shemal said in a small voice. "I have no skills, no money, not even clothes that are my own—"

"And all of that can and will change in time— probably a very short time—because those are all little things. I know they seem big to you, and I respect why, but to me, it matters more that all you see is *me.* Not the High Commander, not the Duke of Fathoms Deep, not forty thousand crowns a year and close ties to the High Throne. If you'd been anyone else when I was dumped at that cottage, I would be dead right now or sold off to a life of slavery and lost forever. At best, someone might have helped only after I agreed to pay a generous reward. You risked literally everything to save me, without asking for anything in return, though you had more reason than most to leave me to suffer. So please, stop worrying. Money and clothes are easy things to come by. You offer things infinitely more precious and hard to find."

Shemal nodded, hand trembling faintly as he finally opened the box.

The first item was a signet ring that exactly matched Lesto's, save the inside where Shemal's name was carved. Technically, such a ring should only be given after they were married, but as Sarrica had said—Lesto's mind was made up. The marriage was a formality in the end.

The remaining items were earrings, since Farlanders put far more stock in their piercings than the rings favored by most of the empire.

He'd consulted with Jader before having them made, and though he'd seen excellent sketches, they didn't compare to the real thing: a pair of gold triple hoops threaded with beads made from black pearls, opals, and teal topaz.

He'd never seen Shemal's eyes light up quite like that. "I don't think these are a necessary item," he said hoarsely and immediately set the box down to remove the cheap hoops already in his ears. "Can I really wear them?"

The anxiety Lesto had been carefully ignoring bled away beneath a hot rush of happiness and affection. The man was elated by earrings and completely ignored the ring that granted him damn near the power of a king, and he worried over the way Lesto gave him things. "You'd better wear them. I commissioned them explicitly for you. I hope I got them right, but if something is wrong, blame Jader."

Shemal laughed as he hooked them in place, fingers working deftly to secure the backings. "They're perfect." He shook his head to make them sway and glitter. He smiled shyly. "How do they look?"

Lesto looked at the earrings, the signet still in the box, and smiled with every scrap of adoration only Shemal had ever inspired. "I think they're perfect."

"Thank you," Shemal said and stepped in to kiss Lesto deep and slow, fingers skating over his body, drawing out delicate shivers. "One of these days, I will have a proper gift for you."

"Wear nothing but those earrings and I'll call it even, but as always, I have a running list of people you are more than welcome to punch. Don't forget your ring."

"I'm trying to leave bad habits like punching people behind," Shemal said with a laugh and brushed another kiss across his mouth before stepping back and returning to the jewelry box. He pulled out the ring, smiled as he looked at Lesto. "It's exactly like yours."

"Yes," Lesto said, anxiety returning full force. "It's a trifle early, but after all the delightful near-death adventures we've faced lately, I'd rather you have it now. But if you thought 'my lord' was bad, you are going to hate that everyone will now skip right to 'Your Grace.'

Shemal's mouth dropped open, eyes widening. "But—" He dropped the ring, stared at it, then picked it up. "I guess I really should have figured that out."

"You can refuse," Lesto said slowly. "You aren't obligated to marry—" Shemal's kiss was hard and biting that time, and the nails that scraped along the back of Lesto's neck did nothing to help him remember what they were talking about when Shemal finally drew back. "I realize this is all a bit fast."

"I've moved around aimlessly my whole life," Shemal said. "My mother insists I've wasted most of it.

But the ocean has patterns that no one else can see, and everything washes ashore precisely where she intends." He slid the ring on the third finger of his right hand. "If this is where I've landed, I'm slowly coming to believe it's where I'm meant to be." He frowned slightly, rubbing his thumb over the ring. "Though I admit I don't know the term? The title? For me. I don't think 'Pirate of Fathoms Deep' has quite the right tone."

Lesto disagreed completely. Nothing had ever sounded more perfect. "I certainly think that's appropriate, but your official title is Duchen. You'll be Lord Shemal Arseni, the Duchen of Fathoms Deep."

"Sounds pompous."

"Shut up." Lesto yanked him close and kissed him hard enough he left his own lips bruised. "It's long past time you took me to bed, pirate."

Eyes turning the color of sun-warmed gems, Shemal kissed him as only a plundering pirate could, and dragged him away to bed.

Epilogue

Shemal stretched out where he lay on the settee in his sitting room. It had been his private sitting room since mere days after he'd moved in with Lesto, but two years later, it still amused and baffled him he had his own room with no purpose other than to sit or lay about, and occasionally invite other people to join him.

He certainly had no complaints, though. What was there to complain about in being able to spend an afternoon sprawled on a settee, a book on his chest, a carafe of wine on a nearby table, his only plan for the day to do obscene things to his husband when he returned from the fields.

Not that he always had that much free time, usually he was at Harkenesten working with Allen and Tara on the projects they'd drawn him into: various reformations concerning how Islanders were treated, somehow he was becoming more and more involved in the shipyards, and he would never admit it but he liked helping Tara oversee the various balls and festivals and such the High Throne frequently charged to his care. Shemal still had a great deal to learn, but the life of a pirate had proven more useful to life as a noble than he ever would have thought possible.

As if summoned by his thoughts, familiar footsteps came from the hall, the jangle of armor and sword belt long ago replaced by the click of heels. He heard the barest murmur of voices moments before the door opened.

Shemal smiled as he sat up, absently catching the book he'd already forgotten about. He set it aside as he rose to greet Lesto with a lingering kiss. "How did it go?"

"New field manager seems to be settling in well, and our yields should be better than ever, Pantheon willing. I stopped by the brewery and brought back some new samples to try with dinner."

Shemal grinned. "You say the sweetest things."

Shaking his head slightly, curling his fingers into the folds of Shemal's shirt, Lesto replied, "Say something sweet to me."

"You know much I like you in black pearls," Shemal replied, eyes dropping to the band of them resting snug against Lesto's throat. "Why say when I can do?"

Lesto made a low, rough noise that never failed to elicit shivers. His gray eye turned more silver. "Then *do*, pirate."

Shemal slid his hands down Lesto's chest to the gold buttons of his dark red jacket and undid them slowly, lingering and brushing teasingly with every single one.

"You are being—"

Lesto's words were cut off by a knock at the door. That was Leeta's knock, but she'd only interrupt if they had a guest, and to Shemal's knowledge, they weren't expecting anyone. Lesto looked equally confused—and annoyed—as he called for Leeta to enter.

"Lord Shemal, I am sorry to disturb, but you've a visitor."

"Me?" Shemal asked, growing even more puzzled.

Leeta bowed her head slightly. "Yes, Your Grace. She claims to be your sister, I think, but my Islander is poor, and there was no one around to translate for me."

"My sister," Shemal repeated, bafflement starting to turn into annoyance. He had about twenty sisters, but he only knew one who would travel across an entire continent and find her way to his doorstep even though she didn't speak anything but Islander. The question was *why*. "Does she have freckles, a squashed-looking nose, and sounds incredibly bossy no matter what she's saying?"

Leeta's mouth twitched. "She is quite commanding, Your Grace."

"Send her to me," Shemal said, pressing his fingers to his temples. "So I can kill her."

Leeta laughed as she left.

"So I'm guessing you didn't invite your sister to visit?" Lesto asked with a smile.

"If I were dumb enough to try inviting *one* sibling, it wouldn't be her, and about fifty would show up anyway. I wrote to ask her one question..." Dawning realization and horror swept through him. He'd sent her the letter because she was the one who handled such matters now that their mother had withdrawn. He'd wanted her to reply in a damned letter, not come see him!

"Shemal, are you all right?" Lesto asked. "You look like you're about to collapse."

"I *am* about to collapse," Shemal replied, but before either of them could say more, the door flew open and his sister walked in like a queen, a harried-looking Leeta a few paces behind her.

Shemal scowled. *"You're upsetting Leeta and being rude, Kemal."*

Kemal tossed her hair. *"I don't need to be led—"*

"Apologize or I'll lead your face into the wall!"

"Fine," Kemal said with a huff. She turned to Leeta and said in thick, halting informal Harken, *"My apologize."*

"No apologies necessary," Leeta demurred before turning to Lesto. "Shall I bring tea?"

"Please," Lesto said.

Shemal was still scowling at Kemal. *"What are you doing here?"*

"You wanted children. I had two recently that are perfect. I have brought them."

"My letter said we were going to start thinking *about it, and for you to ask* discreetly *if anyone would be willing. In no language does that translate to you bringing us children!"*

Kemal huffed again, planting her hands on her hips. *"If I left the matter to move at your pace, the children would be twenty before you adopted them! I have twins, now four months old—"*

"Four months!" Shemal howled, throwing his arms up. *"You should not be traveling with* children who are only four *months old, how much seawater* have you been drinking, *you have the brains of a waterlogged Mainlander!"*

Kemal rolled her eyes and turned to look at Lesto, gesturing with both arms toward Shemal.

Lesto grinned and nodded.

Shemal gave them a withering look. "Oh, no, my husband and my sister are not allowed to silently communicate about how ridiculous you think I'm being." He repeated the words in Islander, which only earned him another huff, though Kemal did smile, too. *"If Lesto gets angry with me for such a presumption—"*

"What presumption? You wanted to adopt

children, these children are your blood." She looked at Lesto again, a little bit of predator in her smirk. Turning back to Shemal, she said, *"He looks far too pretty and fit to be one of those tiresome sort who thinks children are only worthy if they are the blood of both parents. I know you're a sandhead, Shem-Shem, but you're not so dried out you'd tolerate that."*

"Do not call me that," Shemal replied. *"You're right, he doesn't have a problem with children not being his blood. That's not the point. The point is we haven't discussed it yet, I haven't asked him if he'd approve—"*

"You keep saying my name, so I feel I should be part of this conversation," Lesto interjected, brows lifting as Shemal's face burned.

Kemal gave the sigh of the long-suffering and unappreciated. *"The children were coming with Rushia, I came ahead to make certain this was in fact your home. I'll be back."* She spun neatly on her heal, the long, heavy braids of her hair flying about, and left as imperiously as she had arrived.

Lesto looked at the door as it closed then turned to Shemal. "What in the world is going on?"

"Um." Shemal swallowed, fingers curling and uncurling. "I never should have written a letter to my stupid sister, that's what. Argh." He pressed the heels of his hands to his forehead. That letter had taken him three days of agonizing and second-guessing and triple checking every word to make certain he'd written them correctly. This was not how he'd wanted this discussion to happen.

"Shemal," Lesto said gently, closing the space between them and pulling his hands down, holding them firmly. "What's wrong?"

Shemal took a deep breath and let it out slowly. "No matter what I say or how I say it, I'm going to come off looking like a scheming, manipulative ass—"

Lesto drowned him out with a laugh. "You could not be a manipulative schemer if you tried. Stop fretting and stalling and tell me what this is all about."

"All right," Shemal said, and took another deep breath before he finally explained, "You've been mentioning children more and more. I have no taste for hiring a dame. That meant we'd likely adopt. I..." he stared at their clasped hands. "I thought maybe we could adopt some Islander children. But I didn't want to ask without knowing if anyone from my family or community would even agree to let the Variago embarrassment adopt their children. So I wrote to Kemal and asked her to *quietly* look into the matter for me." His shoulders slumped. "Now here she is on our doorstep—

"She brought us *children?*" Lesto gaped. "That's why you mentioned children earlier, only four months old, right? I can't believe it."

Shemal flinched. "I'm sorry, I thought I was far enough away she'd behave. I'd never presume—" He broke off with a soft, startled gasp as Lesto's hands cupped his head.

"You're quite endearing when you're flustered," Lesto said with a smile. "Also you worry for nothing; to be perfectly honest I took it as a given we'd be adopting Islander children, be it from the Islands themselves or orphans abandoned on the Mainland. I admit I was not expecting to adopt two of them today." He kissed Shemal softly, sending a warm, lazy shiver down his spine. "But I'm not inclined to complain."

MEGAN DERR

Shemal stared at him, blinked. "You're not?"

"No, though it is a bit sudden so there will be some scrambling to rearrange the house and our schedules to accommodate children. Babies, at that. I had assumed we'd start with children a little bit older." He smiled and pulled away, striding to the door in that High Commander way of his. He pulled it open—then drew back as Leeta came in bearing a tea tray, another servant behind her holding an additional plate of food since Lesto and Shemal alone tended to eat nigh-obscene amounts. "Leeta, good, I need to pull you and some of the other staff from your regular duties."

Leeta set the tea down then turned, folding her hands in her long apron. "Whatever you wish, Your Grace."

"Shemal's sister, Kemal, has brought two children that we intend to adopt. A bit sooner than expected, but I think we can manage. Would you see the nursery and such are made ready?"

Leeta's normally blank expression turned into one of excitement, a grin overtaking her face. "Congratulations, Your Graces. Of course, we'll take care of everything." She strode over to Lesto and gave him a quick hug, then did the same to Shemal before motioning sharply to the other servant and heading briskly from the room.

The door had not even had a chance to close before Kemal returned, carrying a baby and trailed by a handsome young man—significantly younger, Shemal noted with a twitch of lips—carrying a second baby. *"You said you were bringing two children, not three."*

Kemal rolled her eyes and ignored him, instead going up to Lesto and offering the baby she held.

Lesto took the baby with the ease of someone familiar, which didn't really surprise Shemal though it maybe should have as he'd never seen Lesto around babies in the time they'd been together. *"Thank you,"* he said in Islander.

Beaming, Kemal patted his arm then motioned for her lover to hand the second child to Shemal, who took the baby and sat on the settee. *"Have you named them yet?"*

"Of course not; I have some manners," Kemal said with a toss of braids. *"I'll stay to feed them, of course."*

Shemal groaned. *"No, you're not staying that long."*

Kemal crossed the room and kicked his ankles, huffing when he yelped. *"Do not wake them! I will stay, and you will show me around your ridiculous, but pretty home. I want to go to the palace, as well. Is it true the beached fish from Belarigo who flounced off like you is in charge of the imperial army? Do they know he's not a Mainlander? I want to wear pretty jewels like yours, and I want suitable clothes."*

"Like I would fail to dress my sister well while she is a guest in my home," Shemal replied. *"Unlike you, I have plenty of manners."*

"If you say so," Kemal said, and turned so she could watch Lesto as well as Shemal. Grinning in that evil elder sister way of hers, she said, *"He's quite pretty. Does he have Islander leanings or is he dull like you?"*

Shemal lifted his eyes to the ceiling. *"He's like me and even if he wasn't, I'm not sharing him with my sister, you bottom-feeder."*

"Better a bottom-feeder than a head full of sand," she retorted.

Before Shemal could give that the reply it

deserved, Lesto cut in with a soft chuckle. "The way you two bicker is more than enough to mark you as siblings, though you do resemble each other, too. What are you bickering about this time?"

"Kemal insists on staying to nurse the children as long as they need. She is listing off everything she wants me to do while she is here, including buy her clothes and jewels to wear." His mouth curved in a mischievous smile. "She is also quite set on going to the palace."

"Perhaps when the children are a little older," Lesto replied. "Unless Sarrica finds out, in which case we'll be going the moment he does."

Shemal laughed and repeated all he'd said to Kemal. She smiled when he was done, then leaned down to kiss his cheek. *"You look happier than I've ever seen you, little brother. Now I am going to find your serving woman and see about finding a room. We are quite tired. The babies were fed recently, so they'll be fine for a little while. I'll come find them when they need to be fed again."*

"Do you need me to come translate?"

Kemal scoffed and waved a hand at him. Crossing to Lesto, she leaned up and kissed his cheek as well. *"My brother seems to have chosen well, even if you are a Mainlander."* Giving them both a lofty nod, she swept grandly from the room again, her lover casting them a sheepish smile before he followed her out.

Lesto sat next to Shemal on the settee, his eye silvery and bright, a smile on his face. "I had no idea you were the quiet one in your family."

"No one ever believes me when I say that," Shemal said with a laugh. He looked down at the baby in his arms, who fussed briefly before settling into sleep once more. "We'll have to come up with names."

"We can discuss it tonight," Lesto said, and leaned over to kiss him softly. "If you were plotting to finally outstrip me on the matter of gift-giving, I concede the victory."

Shemal laughed again. "I will remind you of those words when we're interrupted or woken up for the third time in a row by wailing children."

"Better than being woken by wailing soldiers and imperials," Lesto replied, and kissed him again, long and slow, leaving behind a sweet ache. "Come along, pirate; let's see if the nursery is ready yet."

"Yes, Commander," Shemal said with a grin as he stood and followed Lesto from the room.

Fin

Coming 2017 – *The Heart of the Lost Star*

Kamir is on the verge of losing everything. Knowing full well he can't meet the ultimatum his parents have issued, he instead finally puts in motion his plans to live completely independent of them. His plans are interrupted, however, by the unexpected return of his despised ex-husband—and thrown even further into upheaval when he ends up comforting the man he has secretly loved for years.

Jader may not know where he comes from, but he knows where he belongs and what he wants—until he helps rescue some stranded travelers, one of whom look almost exactly like Jader, throwing his life and everything he thought he knew into tumult. Scared and overwhelmed, Jader flees—and lands unexpectedly in the arms of a man he's always seen, but never really noticed.

About the Author

Megan is a long time resident of queer romance, and keeps herself busy reading, writing, and publishing it. She is often accused of fluff and nonsense. When she's not involved in writing, she likes to cook, harass her wife and cats, or watch movies. She loves to hear from readers, and can be found all over the internet.

meganderr.com
patreon.com/meganderr
pillowfort.io/maderr
meganderr.blogspot.com
facebook.com/meganaprilderr
meganaderr@gmail.com
@meganaderr

Made in United States
North Haven, CT
01 April 2022

17758314R00125